Also by Michael R. Davidson

Harry's Rules

Incubus

The Incubus Vendetta

Caliphate – The Inquisitor and the Maiden

Krystal

The Dove (coming soon)

By Michael R. Davidson and Kseniya Kirillova

In the Shadow of Mordor

CALIPHATE
RETRIBUTION

BY

MICHAEL R. DAVIDSON

Retribution

MRD Enterprises, Inc.
PO BOX 1000
Mount Jackson, VA 22842-1000
mrdenter@shentel.net

Library of Congress Control Number: TXu001815215_
(LOC under title "Caliphate")
ISBN 978-0-692-24170-7

Cover illustration

U.S. Department of Energy photograph of XX-14 FIZEAU, an 11 kiloton tower shot fired September 14, 1957 at the Nevada test site

Title plate: Seal for the Tribunal in Spain
Illustration of Boabdil from an 1899 engraving by Lalauze

Printed and bound in the United States of America.

First printing 2014
Second printing 2016

This book is dedicated to the memory of
Comisario Principal Alberto Elías
Cuerpo Nacional de Policía De España

&

My dear friends "Gordi," "Gabi," Bob,
and the late and sorely missed
Nicolás Valero

To the Reader

In the development of this novel the author was inspired in part by historical events connected with the Inquisition in Renaissance Spain, the Iran-Iraq War, and modern day Spain.

I write cloak and dagger stories, and that was my intention when I started work on a book I originally entitled "Caliphate." Somehow, I know not at what point, the colorful history of Spain asserted itself, and I ended up with the "cloak and sword" swashbuckler published as "Caliphate – The Inquisitor and the Maiden" separately. There are important continuities between the earlier book and this one, and for this reason a reading of the earlier work will explain much about the Macías character and certain aspects of the present story.

I could not have written this book were it not for my deep and abiding admiration for Spain and its people. There is no country on earth with a more exciting history, from the days of the ancient Ibero tribes, to the Roman conquest, to the relatively short rule of the Visigoths whose unfortunate King Rodrigo was defeated by the Moors in 711 AD. The Moors created the fabled Muslim realm of *Al Andaluz*, and they reigned for seven centuries, imbedding their vocabulary and customs into Iberian culture. After centuries of battle, the Spanish finally completed their re-conquest (*La Reconquista*) of their peninsula in the fateful year of 1492, when this story begins.

It is my hope that my friends in Spain, many of them former members of the *Cuerpo Nacional de Policía*, will forgive my having used them as models for certain characters in this book. They will be easily recognizable to those who know them.

Worthy of special mention is the extraordinary person upon whom the principal character, Macías, is based. This was my dear friend *Comisario Principal* Alberto Elías whose untimely death in 1993 saddened us all and robbed Spain of her finest police officer. Alberto was an extraordinary man, full of energy and enthusiasm. I will always be grateful to him for his many kindnesses to me, for his courage, sharp wit, and tremendous sense of humor. Had it not been for him, my time in Spain would have been much less rewarding. Rest in peace, my dear friend.

MRD
New Market, VA
2014

ABU ABDULLAH (BOABDIL)

"It is not the critic who counts, not the man who points out how the strong man stumbled, or where the doer of deed could have done better. The credit belongs to the man who is actually in the arena; whose face is marred by the dust and sweat and blood; who strives valiantly; who errs and comes short again and again; who knows the great enthusiasms, the great devotions and spends himself in a worthy course; who at the best, knows in the end the triumph of high achievement, and who, at worst, if he fails, at least fails while daring greatly; so that his place shall never be with those cold and timid souls who know neither victory or defeat."

THEODORE ROOSEVELT (Paris, Sorbonne, 1910)

MICHAEL R. DAVIDSON

Lighting the Fuse[1]

The End of the World, January 3, 1492

"Allah O'Akbar!"

Abu Abdullah hunched in the saddle shivering beneath his heavy cloak in the frigid wind that swept down from the winter-whitened Sierra Nevada. A few hours earlier he had surrendered the city of Gharnata, known to the Christians as Granada, the last Moorish stronghold in Spain, to Fernando and Isabella, their Most Catholic Majesties. He could still see the gleam of triumph in the King's dark, clever eyes.

Now he halted his richly caparisoned horse, and the shivering, lachrymose caravan that stretched behind paused at the entrance to the long, narrow valley of the Alpujarras, known to the Moors as the Hills of the Sun and the Moon. Until this moment he had dared not look back at the Alhambra's still visible rose-colored ramparts for fear that his soul would tear itself from his body to return to the enchanted halls and gardens that had been his home. He expelled a long, trembling sigh that expressed unspeakable melancholy and shame, and burst into bitter tears.

---

[1] Excerpted from "The Inquisitor and the Maiden," Michael R. Davidson, 2013

"Allah O'Akbar," he sobbed.

His mother, the fierce Sultana Aisha al-Hurra, riding in a litter by his side looked upon her disconsolate son with disgust and spat, "Weep! Weep like a woman for the land you could not defend like a man!"

She stabbed an accusing henna-dyed finger at him.

"Shame," she shrieked so that all could hear, "shall be your heritage.

Abu Abdullah did not respond but only turned his horse away from the Sabika hill. He would never see it again.

The Alhambra, Granada – Spring 1575

The music of the fountains pleased the old man who reclined on a cushioned litter carefully placed inside the pink marble pillars of a shaded patio. The position afforded him the most comprehensive view of the sun-dappled Court of the Lions at the heart of the Alhambra. The Andalusian spring had come to Granada under a clear, azure sky, and the fragrance of jasmine and orange blossoms lingered thickly in the still cool air of mid-morning.

The old man was dressed in robes after the Muslim tradition and for this day had demanded that his head be wrapped in a turban. He sensed the spirits of the past that lingered in the exquisite structure, artists beyond compare who had created and inhabited this jewel, this ruby set upon the Sabika hill of Granada as the poet had described it.

One of his grandsons, in fact his namesake, 14-year-old Miguel, sat cross-legged on the flagstones beside the litter, his face bright in anticipation of one of the old man's stories.

"Tell me again the story of Aisha, Grandfather."

The old man, Miguel Fernandez, was known as "the Knight of Granada," a title he detested and one that had receded into the dimness of history even during his own lifetime. He was now entering his eightieth year.

He placed a gnarled, brown hand on the boy's fine, dark hair and smiled his approval.

"This is a story you must never forget, my boy, and one you must pass on to your own children. In my veins and in yours flows the blood of two royal houses as unlike as oil and water. My birth was intended to reconcile the two, or so proclaimed my illustrious father." His expression turned sour when he pronounced the word. "That was the sort of pabulum he and his pious wife dished out."

The old man closed his eyes, and through the distance of the years conjured up the dark face of his father, Fernando of Aragon, that most Catholic of Kings. He had a clear memory of the King standing him on a chair in this very palace and examining him as though he were an exotic pet. Miguel had rejoiced with his unfortunate mother when news of the rapacious Fernando's death reached Granada. There was much blood on the King's hands, and Miguel fervently hoped that Shaitan had reserved a special place for him in Hell.

"Your grandmother was called Aisha in honor of her own fierce grandmother. She was but thirteen when my grandfather, Abu Abdullah, whom the Christians call 'Boabdil' and whom we call 'al zogoybi,' the unfortunate, was driven from his kingdom. Fernando of Aragon espied her among Abu Abdullah's household and lusted after her for she was more beautiful that the stars and the moon. As the price for permitting Abu Abdullah to go into exile with his entire retinue, Fernando demanded that Aisha remain behind to become his concubine."

Throughout his life the old man had wondered what Queen Isabella 'La Católica' had thought of her royal husband's decision to take the young and beautiful daughter of the deposed Abu Abdullah to his bed. Fernando had advertised it as a 'royal duty,' and Miguel Fernandez, his bastard offspring, was to serve as a symbol of reconciliation between Christians and Muslims.

But there was to be no reconciliation. Fernando supported a cruel Inquisition imposed upon the non-Christian inhabitants of Spain, and the inflexible Isabella approved of the inhuman measures taken by Tomás de Torquemada's Dominican inquisitors to "convert" Jews and Muslims to the "True Faith" because she believed *she was saving their souls.*

The old man closed his eyes again, momentarily overcome by the strength of his memories and was brought back to the present by his grandson tugging on his sleeve. He continued the tale.

"My mother, may Allah bless her and keep her, was a saint. She inherited the strength and spirit of her grandmother for whom she was named, Aisha al-Hurra, who ensured that her granddaughter was left with women of Abu Abdullah's royal household to look after her needs. Fernando insisted that she be baptized into the Christian faith, and much was made of this. But the Christian King's hypocrisy was limitless. He always insisted that my mother dress in the Moorish fashion for his connubial visits. The flowing silks and vivid colors aroused his lust."

The old man's eyes glowed for a moment with remembered loathing.

"The Moorish women Abu Abdullah left behind to look after her secretly instructed Aisha in the True Faith. Imagine the pain she must have felt when Fernando tired of her and locked her away in a convent, giving her the name 'Sister Isabel.' The very name of his rabid queen! I was but a lad not much older than you at the time, not much older than she had been when Abu Abdullah abandoned her. I was allowed to visit her but twice each year, on Easter and Christmas.

"Just as she had been instructed in secret in the ways of the True Faith, so was I. The court of

5

Granada escaped the worst ravages of the Holy Inquisition in those days, and my mother saw to it that my education was managed by wise men. I learned to lie to the nosy infidel crows in their black robes. They were easy to fool, as you also have learned, my dear boy. This is the tradition of our family, our true heritage."

The old man raised himself to a sitting position and stared deeply into the boy's eyes.

"Patience is our weapon. You cannot expect victory in your lifetime, or even the lifetimes of your own grandchildren. Your task, your holy duty, is to keep the flame alive and pass it down from father to son. You will acquire wealth, recruit adherents and your power will grow. We are but the spark that ignites a long fuse. One day the enemy will let his guard drop. He will feel secure and he will become careless. Whether it is tomorrow or generations from now, that will be the time to strike."

The sun by now had reached its zenith, and the old man rested his head on the pillows and closed his eyes to nap and soak in the energy of the Andalusian sun and dream of divine retribution.

CHAPTER 1

Aznalcazar, Andalusia, Spain

One-by-one the cars crunched to a stop in the graveled circular drive in front of the white stuccoed hacienda. They had driven slowly up a long, winding graveled drive that passed through an olive grove, the gnarled trunks of the trees, the *oliveros,* attesting to their antiquity and nobility. The cars were all prestige makes, Mercedes, BMW's, a couple of Bentleys. The picturesque estate, set near the banks of the Guadiamar River, comprehended some fifteen thousand hectares northwest of Seville, near the village of Aznalcazar. The main house and outbuildings could not be seen even from the narrow country road that led past the entrance, guarded by an electronic gate and CCTV camera.

The drivers of the cars had names like Toledo, Sevilla, Del Pozo, and Blanco – all referring to places, things, or colors. These were not traditional Spanish family names, but rather typical "Christian" names the "Moriscos," converted Moors, had been forced to adopt if they wished to remain in King Fernando's Spain after 1492. In that august year, Jews and moors that refused to renounce their religions were expelled from the country with only what they could carry on their backs. Those less fortunate had simply been murdered. The wealth they left behind was greedily expropriated by the Church, the state and nobles in its favor.

The men in the cars, a dozen in all, each of them prosperous and well respected in their communities and professional fields, came tonight to attend a secret meeting of an ancient society to which they and their fathers and their fathers' fathers had belonged.

Their leader, Miguel Fernandez de Blanco, was prominent in Seville society. He held vast estates throughout Andalusia and as far as Valencia to the north. Those estates made him an immensely wealthy man. At 60 and a widower, Fernandez was a trim, compact man.

He was a great aficionado of *tauromagia,* the art of bull fighting, and was a fixture at Seville's famed *Maestranza.* For a matador to exert such control over a huge *toro de lidia*, a fighting bull, required years of training, strict discipline, immense talent, and a complete mastery over fear, traits that defined Fernandez, as well. Like the matador, Miguel Fernandez both respected his opponent and lived to bring it to its knees.

Few aficionados of the bullring, he was certain, realized that their cries of "*Olé, olé*" were an unwitting reference to "Allah."

He loved the land, this Andalusia but longed for it to be cleansed and returned to his vision of the Islamic purity it had once known, and now, at last, after generations of waiting and planning, he possessed the means to do just that.

At this time of year the Muslim sunset prayer, the *Maghrib*, commenced a few minutes before six p.m., followed immediately by the *Isha*, the prayer of nightfall when the first stars appeared, and his visitors had made sure to arrive before the appointed hour.

They gathered in a special room in the *Mudejar* style. All had quickly discarded their Western clothing in favor of long, silk robes. The room was oriented toward the *Quiblah*, the direction of the *Ka'abah* in Mecca. A *Mihrab*, a niche in the wall, indicated the direction of the Holy City. At the appointed hour, all faced the *Quiblah* and raised their hands, palms uplifted, as they chanted *Allahu Akbar* to formally begin the prayer and then recited the *Fatihah*, the first chapter of the *Qur'an*.

At the close of the *Isha*, the robed men sat while Fernandez rose to speak.

"My brothers, for the ages through which our honored families have suffered and survived and nurtured the Faith, the reward is at hand. An act of *jihad* must be carried out to convince the infidels that they have no choice but to return our ancestral lands so painfully stolen from us. As civilized men, we recognize that this is regrettable, but without a demonstration of our power and our will, nothing can be accomplished. Our resolve must be firm.

"Islam has fallen upon hard times. Wherever one might look in the lands of the Prophet, blessed be His name, one sees war, poverty, ignorance, cruelty, cupidity, and corruption. This is not the Islam of *Al Andaluz*.[2] We gathered here have never been privileged to make the *hadj*, although in our hearts we all have circled the *Ka'abah*. But I say to you that Allah, blessed be His name, knows our hearts and sees in them a purity of spirit that has been absent for too long in the mosques of the East.

"In the West they are fond of saying that Islam needs a Reformation. What they refuse to recognize is that *Al Andaluz* was the seat of our Reformation. And I say to you that if we do not act now, our ideals will be forever crushed under the tide of fundamentalism that threatens to overwhelm the Faith. I remind you that we are not the Taliban or Al Qaeda.

"We represent the apogee of Islamic **civilization**, and once our victory is secured our example will inspire the entire Islamic world."

Fernandez pushed a button on the remote

---

[2] The Arabic name given to Muslim Andalusia.

control he held in his hand, and a large high-definition flat screen descended from the ceiling behind him.

"Let me explain the logic of our plan."

The screen lit up with a map of Europe.

"It begins with demographics. No culture can maintain itself if its fertility rate falls below two children per couple. This is simple math."

He swept his arm toward the screen.

"There is no country in Western Europe today that has a fertility rate of more than 1.8. In fact, across the entire European Union the rate is 1.4. In the case of Spain, it is only 1.1. These facts portend a watershed change in Europe.

"That change will be due entirely to south-to-north migration – Islamic migration. Since 1990, Islamic immigration has accounted for ninety percent of all population growth in Europe.

"It is believed that in southern France there are now more mosques that Christian churches. In the Netherlands 50% of all newborns are said to be of Muslim parents. In less than two decades, half of the population of that country will be Muslim. According to one report, by 2025 one-third of ALL children born in Europe will be Muslim.

"The question is who will control Islamic Europe? We see extremists everywhere, and they take advantage of the low economic and educational levels of the immigrant population. This is not the Islam that we know or desire. This is not the Islam we want to see controlling

Europe."

A murmur of assent ran through his listeners.

Fernandez continued, "Before this can happen, before the fanatics can gain control, *Al Andaluz* must be reborn as the center of Islamic thought."

He pressed a button on the remote, and the map of Europe was replaced by a map of Spain. On it a jagged line was drawn from Huelva on the southwest coast to Valencia on the east coast.

"All Muslims now in Spain will be invited to join us here. We will not insist on the forced conversion of the Christians and others now living here and who wish to remain, thus demonstrating to the world our humanity and tolerance."

He clicked the remote control again.

On the screen flashed a photo showing a large gray, barrel-shaped object with Cyrillic lettering stenciled on its side.

A hushed awe gripped the room.

"And this, my brothers, is the means to achieve our end. When I acquired it I was still uncertain about how or even whether I could use it, but Spain's capitulation to simple terrorism after M-11 convinced me that the blood of Fernando of Aragon and the Conquistadors has become thin and weak. It has taken a long time to shape the plan and find someone with the requisite technical skills to carry it out, but now after so many centuries we are ready to strike."

CHAPTER 2

Tehran, The Islamic Republic of Iran

Major Firouz Shirazi could not deduce the reason he had been summoned an hour earlier from his laboratory at the military base in Parchin 50 kilometers southwest of Tehran and frantically searched his memory for anything, any infraction he or his family might have committed that could have aroused the interest of the intelligence service or the mullahs.

Fear churned through him as the driver of the shiny black Mercedes turned onto the long ramp feeding into the heavy west bound traffic on the Hemmat Highway that traversed central Tehran. All the same, he was grateful the car had not turned north onto Highway 2, which would have meant his destination was the tall, deceptively modern multi-story building that housed the operational arms of VEVAK, the *Vezarat-e Ettela'at va Amniat-e Keshvar* or the Ministry of Intelligence and Security of the Islamic Republic of Iran. Instead, he was being driven to the Ministry of Intelligence and Security headquarters where the Minister himself presided.

Just a short few miles in the distance the 435 meter tall Milad Telecommunications Tower pushed imposingly into a clear, blue sky, like the stiff finger of an imam emphasizing a Quranic verse. The tower had been completed only a few years earlier on the site of the city's World Trade Center.

He wished his destination were one of the expensive restaurants at the top of the tower rather than the complex of large white buildings now coming into view on the left of the highway – the headquarters complex of MOIS. Until 1979 the highly guarded compound had been the headquarters of the Shah's intelligence service, SAVAK, a pre-revolutionary institution that had united Iranians in hatred. But its reputation had grown even darker since it had been taken over by VEVAK. Many who entered never left. Everyone had heard the grisly tales about what went on in the holding cells before prisoners were transported to the infamous Section 209 of Evin Prison where torture and death awaited with the certainty of the rising sun.

Shirazi's thoughts raced. His work on the Iranian nuclear weapons program was highly confidential, so the ministry would naturally have a file on him. But to have been drafted into the program in the first place by the Revolutionary Guard surely meant that he was considered trustworthy.

That he was trusted at all was because his elder brother, Majid, had martyred himself as a *Basij* during the Iran – Iraq War. His body had never been returned to the family, but they had received a fine certificate attesting to Majid's heroism. As a member of a martyr's family, Firouz had received benefits, most particularly educational opportunities, and perhaps thanks to what he had learned in his father's modest machine shop, he had turned to engineering, graduating with honors from university and then joining the Air Force. Flying high above the perverse politics of the imams had imparted at least a transitory sense of freedom, but his talents as an engineer had attracted the interest of the nuclear program managers, and he had not been at the controls of an aircraft in over a year.

Within moments of leaving the highway, the big car passed through the main security checkpoint and glided to a stop in a plaza that lay between two large, square buildings. A uniformed enlisted man hurried down the steps to escort him directly to an austere office where Aref Zarin waited behind a desk. Zarin stood to greet him with a welcoming smile. The three stars on his shoulder boards advertised his rank as a *sarhang tamam*, or full colonel, in the Revolutionary Guards Corps.

Shirazi, uncertain of the protocol, snapped to attention and saluted the surprisingly blond haired Zarin. His beard was so light it was barely noticeable from a distance.

The Colonel chuckled softly and stepped around his desk to embrace a mystified Shirazi.

"Salaam Aleikom, Peace be with you, Major."

He introduced himself as VEVAK's head of southern European operations, and Shirazi wondered what the Colonel was doing here at Headquarters.

Shirazi managed to provide the time-honored response, and Zarin stepped back to look him up and down, frankly appraising Shirazi's slim figure and dark skin, a significant contrast from his own white complexion.

Apparently satisfied, the Colonel adopted a friendly tone, "You have been selected for a singular honor, Major Shirazi, one that would make your martyred brother proud. Please follow me. There is someone who wishes to meet you."

Shirazi self-consciously adjusted his blue Air Force uniform and followed the Colonel out of the office to an elevator that whisked them to the top floor. Zarin led him along a bare corridor to an ornate olive wood door where he knocked softly.

"Enter," a voice rasped from within.

Waiting inside were two men, one of which, sharp-eyed behind wire-rimmed glasses, with a neatly trimmed salt and pepper beard, wore the black robes and white turban of a Mullah. Shirazi instantly recognized him: Heydar Moslehi, the recently appointed head of VEVAK. Zarin introduced the second, a thin, swarthy man, short of stature with thick dark hair and a beard that was little more than stubble covering his cheeks, as Mohammad-Reza Iravani, head of VEVAK's Directorate of Overseas Affairs.

This office, in contrast to the generally modest décor of the building boasted a rich Persian carpet and comfortable furniture. An imposing desk sat near the back wall. This must be Moslehi's office.

Iravani raked Shirazi with cold, analytical eyes. Although he had never met him Shirazi knew his reputation as one who brooked no compromise or compassion, who knew no limits and refused to accept failure. Utterly ruthless, Iravani had headed VEVAK's foreign operations for years, dispatched assassins, financed Hezbollah and other terrorist organizations. He had watched with satisfaction as the Islamic Republic's enemies were tortured and then killed or hunted down abroad and murdered.

Moslehi left immediately, but his presence and the fact that the meeting was taking place in his office put the imprimatur and blessing of the Supreme Ruler, the Ayatollah Ali Khameini, on whatever it was they had summoned Shirazi to do.

Iravani invited them to sit. His gaze still dissecting Shirazi, he began to speak, "Major, I believe that you are familiar with the Soviet RS-117 nuclear landmine ..."

CHAPTER 3

Madrid, Spain

"... the French are more talkative; the Spanish more quiet, since they learned to dissimulate better." Ptolemy

The Spanish have a saying, "You can't trust anybody until you've eaten with them three times," and so it is over food that the real business is done in Madrid. Deputy Chief of Station Robert Strachey, therefore, without hesitation accepted *Comisario Principal,* or Chief Inspector Alberto Macías's invitation to lunch at one of their favorite haunts near the Puerta del Sol. In fact, Strachey welcomed any opportunity to escape the seedy offices the CIA inhabited on the top floors of the American Embassy on *Calle de Serrano.* The aging granite and glass eyesore stood in sharp contrast to the elegant Spanish architecture at the top of Madrid's glitziest shopping street. The utilitarian concrete barriers that had been placed around the embassy promised little protection and only added to the building's depressing ugliness.

At 44, the native of Canton, North Carolina, now a veteran of fifteen years with the CIA and two divorces from women who had found it impossible to compete with his profession, was feeling restless and at loose ends in pleasant, but boring Madrid. His mountain home upbringing had instilled within him an independence of spirit, and his collegiate career as a star tight end for the Tarheels taught him to take chances. Unfortunately, he had found little in Spain thus far that called for these traits, and with Christmas fast approaching things were even slower than usual. Lunch with the *Comisario Principal* was a welcome diversion.

He had discovered his most competent and reliable Spanish ally in the modest person of Macías, who had recently been named to head the *Unidad Central de Información Exterior,* known as UCIE, in charge of foreign intelligence operations, which these days meant that he was primarily concerned with terrorist activities. Strachey had worked hard to become his friend.

After sharing an excellent lunch Alberto waived off desert, which suited Strachey who had happily adopted the manly Spanish custom of coffee and cigars, and perhaps a short glass of Galician *orujo,* following a meal. Both ordered coffee and waited in silence for it to be brought to the table. Throughout the meal the Spaniard had limited conversation to the friendly chit-chat in which the Spanish excel. Strachey anticipated that now he would reveal what he really wanted to talk about and waited patiently for his friend to get to the point.

After the waiter had placed the strong *café solo* in small, white cups on the table, Macías's voice became so hushed that Strachey had to lean close to catch his words amidst the clatter of the restaurant.

"I need a favor, Vop."

They spoke in crisp Castilian Spanish. Strachey's name was Bob, but the Spanish encountered a universal impediment when trying to pronounce a name that was a palindrome beginning and ending with a consonant that their language ambiguously allowed them to pronounce as a "V" or a "B" or anything in between. Sometimes they gamely tried a variation that sounded like "Vov," but they never got it right. It was a mystery to Strachey why they didn't just call him 'Roberto.'

"What kind of favor?" Personal favor, professional favor? Sometimes it was hard to separate the two where the Spanish were concerned.

"I need some help with a new contact."

Macías's use of the personal pronoun 'I' signaled to Strachey that he should prepare for a pitch. The National Police operated on a limited budget, and they suffered under the delusion that the CIA was rolling in money and delighted in passing it around. It wouldn't be the first time they had asked the Agency to bankroll something for them. Or it could be access to the Agency's arsenal of arcane technology they were after.

"I'm listening."

Macías read the caution in Strachey's eyes, and quickly added, "It's not what you think. I've come across someone who claims to have important information, but I don't have the resources to confirm it. I would be grateful if your people could help."

"I'm still listening. Do you want us to box him for you?" The Agency term for a polygraph examination.

"Maybe something more." The sly Spaniard dropped his bombshell. "He's Iranian, a military officer, in fact, the air attaché at their embassy here in Madrid."

Strachey managed to keep his face expressionless, but excitement thrilled up and down his spine like Fred Astaire tapping across a vaudeville stage. He and Macías were too familiar with one another for the Spaniard not to know that he had captured the American's full attention with mention of the Iranian.

"Keep talking."

Alberto smiled thinly, knowing he had struck home.

"We keep the bastards under observation, of course, especially after M-11," a reference to the deadly March 11, 2004 bombing of several Madrid train stations. Something flickered briefly behind the Spaniard's eyes that might have been pain or anger. "The Iranians didn't have anything to do with that, of course, but one *Moro* is much like another as far as we're concerned."

Alberto and his colleagues routinely referred to all Muslims as *Moros*, or Moors. Spain had been occupied by Muslim invaders for nearly eight centuries, until they were finally defeated in 1492, and the memory of the long occupation and the *Reconquista* was part of the national psyche. Strachey often wondered how deeply one had to scratch a contemporary Spaniard before finding a trace of an ancient Moor hidden within.

The Iranian Embassy occupied a small compound on *Calle de Jerez* in a residential neighborhood in the northern part of Madrid. The Agency had been after the Spanish for years to work against them, but to no avail. Leery Spanish politicians, especially the party now in power, did not want to be seen aligning themselves with the United States in a showdown with the Islamic world. Now Alberto, incongruously, was inviting CIA participation in a Spanish operation against them.

Strachey flashed an intuition. "Is this an official or an unofficial request, Alberto?"

If it had been official Alberto probably would not have chosen a venue outside his office to make his pitch.

Macías leaned forward with a conspiratorial gleam in his eyes.

"Vop, if the big bosses knew what I was doing they'd skin me and nail my hide to a wall next to a sign saying 'this is what happens when you get too close to the Americans.'"

Strachey had to smile at this reference to the labyrinthine nature of the Spanish intelligence establishment. In his role as Deputy Chief of Station he liaised with the National Police and the Guardia Civil – quite different entities, each with its own history and competing responsibilities. On occasion he also dealt with the standoffish *Centro Nacional de Inteligencia*, a mostly military outfit. Within each service there were individual fiefdoms, and Alberto had his own coterie of allies, mostly men he had grown up with in the service. They didn't always tell their superiors what they were up to, and Strachey had learned to speak only in vague generalities when dealing with the service Chiefs. He knew the real power and the real operations were at Alberto's level.

If what Macías was offering was real, Langley's full attention would suddenly become fixed on Madrid, but Strachey wanted to check it out before getting Washington too excited, and he would have to convince his cautious boss to go along with him. He needed to determine if this was an opportunity or just Alberto selling them some trouble.

"Have you met this guy yourself, Alberto?"

"*Sí*. He approached us."

"Do you trust him?"

The wiry Spaniard gave an Iberian shrug of

his shoulders, a gesture inherently distinct from the well-known Gallic shrug: with the French a shrug conveys a sense of indifference; with the Spanish one always infers that they know more than they are saying.

Alberto cocked an eyebrow at the CIA man. "Trust? Of course not. But that's what I want you to help me determine, isn't it?"

CHAPTER 4

It was nearing 5:30 P.M. by the time Strachey returned to the Embassy and rode the creaking elevator to the down at heels station spaces at the top of the building. Myra, the secretary he shared with Chief of Station Sidney Jones was still at her desk looking impatient to leave, which meant that Jones had not yet left for the day.

Jones had spent his career in Latin America before catching the brass ring that all Latin America field officers desired: assignment to Madrid as Chief of Station. It might seem natural and appropriate to move an LA specialist to Spain, given the similarity of cultures and common language. But the Spanish were thoroughly European, highly sophisticated, and the inheritors of a long, difficult, and proud history. Old line LA field hands like Jones, accustomed to assuming superiority over little brown Spanish-speaking people, often made the mistake of treating the Spanish the same. Relations with the Spanish services suffered as a result.

Jones was in his office, in his shirt sleeves, feet propped on his desk, reading the afternoon papers. He looked up and smiled an easy welcome as Strachey entered. He was in his mid-fifties, short and wiry, with a shock of rapidly graying hair that he could never quite keep under control.

"So how was lunch?"

"Interesting. Let's go to the bubble."

Jones looked up sharply. "It's really THAT interesting?"

"Yup."

Under the glare of overhead florescent lamps in the bubble, a Plexiglas room within a room designed to thwart electronic eavesdropping, Strachey pulled out his notes. The Iranian's name was Firouz Shirazi. He claimed to have worked in Iran's nuclear weapons program, a program covertly supported by the Russians, the code name of which was "Project *Magush*."

Jones' jaw dropped. "The Russians are helping with the Iranian nuclear weapons program? Jeez, that'll set them back on their heels at Langley. Any more surprises?"

"Alberto told me just enough to bait the hook. He said he wanted me to hear for myself what Shirazi has to say. Whatever it is, it's more than he thinks he can handle on his own."

"What do you want to do?" Jones had learned to listen to his deputy.

Strachey mentally crossed his fingers. He liked Jones, but the COS deferred too many decisions to Headquarters and was overly obsequious to the political appointee U.S. ambassador to Spain, a prissy economist that Strachey uncharitably thought was a howling idiot. Taking a deep breath, he said, "Let me meet the guy and get the full story before we say anything to Langley. It'll put us in a better position to make recommendations."

He hesitated for a moment before continuing, "And, Sidney, I also think it's too early in the game to inform the Ambassador."

Jones was sensitive about his reputation as a toady to the Ambassador, and his irritation showed in the red spots that appeared on his cheeks.

"The Ambassador represents the President, Bob," he said, and Strachey held his breath, "but we should probably let Langley decide this one."

*****

First meetings for anybody can be awkward, easy, fateful or inconsequential. But the first meeting between the CIA and a potential intelligence source is always charged with additional dimensions. It could be like the first kiss of tentative lovers or the first round of a prize fight.

For the CIA the first order of business always was to establish *bona fides*.

Strachey turned up the collar of his raincoat against the discomfort of a light December evening shower as he crossed the rain slicked cobblestones of the Plaza Mayor. Strings of multi-colored Christmas lights glowed festively in the shop windows in the arcades that surrounded the broad square. It was hard to reconcile the benign appearance the Spanish landmark presented tonight with the bullfights it had seen in the far distant past, not to mention to excesses of the Spanish Inquisition. The human torches that had illuminated the plaza during that dark period had had little to do with the impending holiday's promise of peace on earth, good will toward men. The Black Legend born of those times would be forever associated with Spain, and one could still glimpse the cruelty buried deeply in the Spanish psyche in the blood sport still practiced at Madrid's *Las Ventas* bull ring.

The evening's earlier mist had graduated to a cold drizzle that promised to intensify, and Strachey paused gratefully under the temporary shelter of the arcade at the southwest corner of the plaza. After a moment he proceeded down the broad steps leading to the picturesque *Calle de Cuchilleros*.

A tapas restaurant was the supremely confident Alberto's idea of a clandestine meeting site. A safehouse would have been better, or even a deserted park, but this was just Alberto displaying the goods before he made the sale. Presumably the wily Spaniard had counter-surveillance deployed. This meeting would be brief, followed by a lengthier one if Strachey was impressed by what he saw and heard.

The narrow, sloping street was lined with *tapas* bars, each specializing in a different over-priced delicacy and Strachey was familiar with the one Macías had chosen. Inside and grateful for the warmth, he shed his coat and draped it over his arm before winding his way through a series of small, stepped galleries that had once served as *bodegas* for food or wine storage. The place was suffused in an amber glow from dim lighting that reflected softly off the ancient stone walls. He finally spotted Alberto seated at a small table against the back wall with Shirazi.

The lanky Iranian wore khaki slacks and a blue shirt with epaulets that might have been part of a uniform. With his dark looks he easily could have passed for Andalusian Spanish. Strachey had just a few seconds to study him before Alberto's look of recognition alerted the Iranian to his arrival.

He didn't look spooked, and that was good. In the restaurant's dim light his deep-set eyes were shaded as he concentrated an appraising gaze on Strachey. What he saw was an athletically built man of average height with wet brown hair parted on the left, clean shaven, with blue eyes. Strachey had chosen informal attire,

Dockers slacks and a green cotton turtleneck under his raincoat, to blend in with the evening crowd.

Neither of them stood as he slid onto the backless wooden bench against the wall next to Alberto so they both faced Shirazi across the plank table.

CHAPTER 5

Alberto made the introductions.

The Iranian continued to study the American without offering his hand. His narrow, dark face was emotionless, but a trickle of perspiration at his hairline betrayed his nervousness. Alberto had used Spanish, and Strachey asked Shirazi if he was comfortable in that language. He just nodded and then looked over his shoulder toward the exit as if he were about to bolt.

"How much time do you have?" asked Strachey.

"I must be back at the embassy before ten PM," Shirazi spoke in a quick burst of ungrammatical Spanish in a raspy, high-pitched voice, a sure sign of anxiety.

"Does anybody know you are here?" Strachey asked his second 'standard question.'

"No."

The American checked his watch and calculated that they had about twenty minutes before the Iranian should leave, just enough time to confirm the basic facts. A full debriefing would require more private conditions. Macías would already have made the arrangements.

Strachey asked his third standard question: "Will anybody miss you tonight?"

"I don't think so." Some certitude in that answer would have been more reassuring.

"What do you want?"

"I want to go to the United States with my family."

Alberto's eyebrows climbed his forehead. *The Iranian really did want to get as far away from Spain as possible.*

"How many in your family?"

"Myself, my wife, and two children."

"They're all here in Madrid with you?"

"Yes."

"Does your wife know you're meeting with us?"

Shirazi shot him an incredulous look. "Of course not. She would be too frightened."

"May I see your documentation?"

More basic tradecraft to establish *bona fides: make sure the person you're meeting is who he says he is.* Of course, Alberto had already verified Shirazi's identity, but Strachey still had to see the documents for himself.

The Iranian slid a salmon colored laminated diplomatic photo I.D. card across the table that identified him as Major Firouz Shirazi, Iranian Air Force attaché. Strachey copied this onto one of the three-by-five note cards he always carried and returned the I.D. card.

"Lots of people want to go to the United States. That doesn't make it automatic. And it won't be easy. You'll have to be resettled with a new name. You'll need money to live on and a job. The organization I represent will expect something in return, and its quality will determine what is done in the end." Lay out the naked facts; establish the rules.

Shirazi's mouth turned down at the corners. "All I want is freedom for me and my family," he said sourly. "Is America not the country of freedom?"

Strachey sighed. Turning people into traitors is the bread and butter of the National Clandestine Services, as the CIA's old Directorate of Operations was now called. They weren't in the business of handing out free airline tickets.

"You're a military officer, an attaché. That means you know all about intelligence, and it also means that you already knew what we would want before you came to this meeting. At our next meeting we will discuss this in detail, and I expect you to describe your access and bring something you think might induce me to go to so much trouble for you."

Alberto Macías sat quietly, his forearms resting on the table, hands clasped. Strachey could see that he was impatient with the mundane questions. He wondered if the Spaniard had expected Shirazi to ask to defect to America. Maybe. It was something the Spanish certainly would not want to handle. But Macías's eyes had widened slightly, perhaps in surprise, when he'd heard the words.

They allowed Shirazi to leave a few moments later. The Iranian Major retrieved his documents and quickly exited the restaurant without looking back.

"Your men are posted outside?" Strachey asked.

"Of course. They'll tail him now to make sure he returns safely to his embassy."

The Spaniard beckoned a waiter to their table and ordered a bottle of *"Jota Bay,"* J&B scotch, a signal that the meeting was not over. Strachey was impatient to get back to the Embassy. There was a lot of work to be done and a flash cable to Headquarters to write.

The waiter returned with a full, green bottle, a small bucket of ice and two tall glasses then bustled away to tend to other customers while Macías did the honors, dropping a few cubes of ice into each glass and then covering them with the light colored whiskey.

"Is that the way you always handle first meetings, Vop?"

"Fictional spooks handle situations by relying on their instincts and luck. Instincts are important, but you have to make your own luck, and real spooks have found that checklists like the one I just took him through are useful. We'll have time to get chummy later." he smiled, "After I've vetted him."   He held up his whiskey. "We'll have to think of a non-alcoholic way to do that, I suppose."

Macías chuckled softly and sipped his scotch.

"What happens now, Vop? Have you briefed Sidney Jones?"

The Spaniards had for years been distrusted by the CIA, and the feeling was mutual. It had cost Strachey considerable effort to win Macías's trust, a trust that did not extend to Sidney Jones.

It was Strachey's turn to smile.

"Don't worry. Sidney's on board with this, providing that Shirazi is who and what he claims to be. Whatever else Sidney may be he recognizes opportunity when he sees it."

"*Bueno.*"

Alberto looked into his glass, "Can you control things on your side?" he asked softly. "There is a great deal at stake and the CIA does not have a reputation for sharing."

For a few beats Strachey said nothing. Something was gnawing at his Spanish friend.

"Why don't you run him yourself, Alberto? I would even recommend it. Bringing the CIA in can be a crap shoot. I'll back out of it right now and fix it with Sidney."

He didn't mean what he said, but was fishing for more information. He thought the Spaniard still was holding something back.

Alberto spread his arms wide in a gesture of helplessness.

"You know why. There are a lot of us in the National Police who would leap at the opportunity, of course, but there are two problems. First, we don't have a lot of experience handling major defectors, and we'd probably have to hand him over to those military assholes at CNI, if we did anything at all, and they would fuck it up."

Strachey said nothing.

Alberto continued, "Second, and more to the point, in the current political climate if I took this matter to my superiors, or even offered Shirazi to the CNI, the politicians at the Moncloa would become as hysterical as old ladies as soon as they heard what he claims to know. To tell them anything would risk the operation." The Moncloa was Spain's Presidential Palace.

This was the second time Macías had hinted that something else was at play here. Given Spain's aversion to offending any Middle Eastern government, if the CIA were to assume responsibility and take the Iranian to the States, the authorities undoubtedly would be relieved.

The Spanish would claim to have known nothing about it.

"One more thing," continued Alberto, confirming Strachey's suspicion. "I want you to promise that you and your people will deal exclusively with me."

So Alberto really was running this one out of his hip pocket.

"I think we can do that, but it'll look strange, almost as if we were running him unilaterally, and there could be some eventual blowback on you, my friend."

Alberto abruptly stood.

"Let's take a walk. There's something more you need to know before you report to Langley. I was going to wait for our next meeting so you could hear it from Shirazi's own lips, but I've changed my mind and I don't even want to whisper it in here." Faint warning bells began to knell in Strachey's mind.

Alberto dropped some cash on the table and started for the exit, pulling on his coat as Strachey followed.

Something heavy was weighing on the Spaniard, something about this case that had rendered him unusually somber. It seemed doubtful to Strachey that the Iranians could have any designs on Spain. They were too focused on destroying Israel, controlling Iraq, and supporting terrorist thugs like Hezbollah in the Middle East, not to mention the little matter of their nuclear weapons program. The nukes were what

Washington was worried about because they didn't have the least idea how to handle the situation, and they were scared shitless that the Israelis might do something precipitous on their own because they had no faith in the current U.S. Administration. If Shirazi really was knowledgeable of Iran's nuclear program, Washington would definitely want in on the game, indeed would be eager to take it over completely and would probably try to do so. A source like Shirazi would be more valuable to the CIA than to the Spanish. Maybe Alberto had decided on his own to let the Americans take over the case.

They shrugged on their coats and stepped back out into the street. The rain had stopped, but the snow-chilled wind from the Guadarrama had lowered the temperature to near freezing and ice crystals now danced in the street lamps' glare. The *Calle de Cuchilleros* was nearly deserted, and they ambled slowly south in the direction of the *Plaza de Segovia* while Alberto told Strachey about his first encounter with Shirazi two days earlier.

CHAPTER 6

Comisario Principal Alberto Macías had been at his desk sifting through reports. He had his hands full trying to uncover Islamist fanatics among the burgeoning Muslim population of Spain that had grown in the span of a few short years from less than a hundred thousand to over a million.

Not far from where he sat, one of the largest mosques in Europe gleamed whitely by the side of the M-30 highway on the eastern edge of Madrid, one of over two hundred mosques now operating in his country. A few years ago the Spanish Government had decided to begin subsidizing the mosques with the idea of reducing the influence of foreign money, specifically Wahabi money from Saudi Arabia. If this had resulted in moderating the amount of jihadist rhetoric, Alberto had not seen it.

The affair with the Iranian had begun

innocently enough when his friend, Gordi, poked his head through Alberto's office door.

"Knock, knock."

Gordi's name was Enrique Castañeda, but the clever Galician's natural rotundity had earned him the "fatso" moniker which he accepted with natural good humor. He had recently been promoted to *Comisario* and put at the head of the *Unidades Periféricas*, the CNP division that managed the *Brigadas Provinciales de Información*, or Provincial Information Brigades.

In sharp contrast to his friend, Alberto was a bespectacled, wiry 45-year-old veteran cop with a short, dark beard that covered his cheeks, an infectious smile when he chose to display it, and a deceptively understated manner.

Without waiting for an invitation Gordi sauntered in and dropped into one of the spindly chairs in front of Alberto's desk. Alberto glanced up in mild alarm as the chair protested Gordi's weighty invasion with loud creaks and an ominous crack.

Annoyed at the interruption, Alberto checked his watch and growled, "It's too early for lunch."

"It's never too early for lunch," Gordi looked placidly down and patted his belly the way some people might caress a favorite pet, "but I've actually come here on business, *Señor Comisario Principal*."

Long Spanish lunches with his friends had become rarities since Alberto's ascension to head the UCIE, and he sorely missed the camaraderie.

Still not quite taking his visitor's words at face value, Alberto crossed his arms and leaned back in his chair.

"You're kidding."

Many had marveled at Gordi's promotion because it often seemed that he considered police work more of an avocation than a profession.

"Now you're hurting my feelings."

The grin that creased Gordi's saturnine face belied his words. It was impossible for Alberto to hurt his feelings.

Alberto sighed, "OK, let's hear it."

"I was out at Nico's country place over the week-end."

He referred to Nicolas Villagas, an old mutual friend who ran a successful cargo airline company, based at Madrid's Barajas International Airport. Villagas was a colorful, extravagant figure. The former fighter pilot had made a pile of money but remained a teenager at heart, driving fast, flashy cars, and cutting a swath through Madrid's exclusive clubs. As a young Air Force officer stationed in Seville, he had fallen in love with a beautiful, raven haired gypsy girl and married her, much to the chagrin of his *Madrileño* parents. They had produced two daughters of incredible beauty and a son who was winning recognition as an artist.

"How is Nico doing, and Carmela?" Villagas' still beautiful wife of nearly 25 years.

"Fine. The paella was terrific. But I didn't

come here to talk about food, *Señor Comisario Principal*."

For some reason Alberto could not fathom, Gordi found his new title highly amusing, but of course Gordi found everything amusing.

Still grinning, Gordi continued, "You know that Nico deals with a lot of interesting people. His airline carries some diplomatic cargo, including for the Iranian Embassy. Well, he met somebody from the Embassy."

"And ...?"

"This is the good part. The guy wants to defect."

"Defect to whom?"

"Us."

Alberto could not conceal his surprise. This must be one of Gordi's jokes. "Spain? Are you serious?"

"*Te lo juro*, I swear."

"Who is he?"

"Nico says he's the Air Attaché, an Air Force officer. Nico says the *Moro* trusts him because they're both pilots."

"*Joder!* Fuck!"

Alberto could envision how such news would be received by his superiors and the Spanish political class. Neither would be enthusiastic about antagonizing the Iranians, not these days. In any case, the CNP didn't have much experience handling defectors. His friend had just handed him a headache and appeared delighted to have done so.

"Gracias, Gordi. Muchísimas gracias."

"Nico said he could arrange a meeting any time you like."

"God knows what Nico told him! I hope he didn't make any promises we can't keep."

Alberto removed his glasses and squinted at Gordi who was now putting dangerous pressure on the back legs of the chair as he rocked back, raising the front legs off the floor, hands folded over his belly.

"You haven't blabbed about this to anyone else have you?"

Gordi did a poor job of pretending he was insulted by the question.

"Of course not. You're the only person in the CNP besides me who knows."

"What about Nico? He's not the most discreet person I know."

"I made him swear on his wife's terrific tits that he would keep it to himself," beamed Gordi.

Sighing heavily as he scanned the stack of reports still awaiting his examination, Alberto rose and grabbed his jacket from the coat hanger behind his desk.

"Let's go see Nico before he does something crazy."

*****

It took them over a half-hour negotiating city traffic to reach Barajas, where they parked in the cargo terminal area where Villagas had his offices.

Alberto prevailed upon Nico to set up a meeting at his office to give the Iranian cover to leave his embassy. Alberto knew that the irrepressible Nico would be delighted to be involved in an espionage operation and he suspected that the dashing airline president already saw himself as a Spanish James Bond. Not surprisingly, he was downcast when Alberto insisted that he not participate in the meeting. Nico pouted, but he left the office after making the introductions.

At almost six feet and thin as a rail, the Iranian towered over Alberto. Like the Spaniard, he sported a closely cropped beard that covered his jaw on a lean, swarthy face dominated by a narrow hook of a nose. His dark brown, almost black eyes seemed uncommonly closely spaced.

Clearly aware of the value of the information, Shirazi eagerly related how he had worked in Iran's nuclear weapons program, the code name of which was "Project *Magush.*" *Magush* meant "magic" in Old Persian, and for many years the secret program had operated behind the façade of a modest building in the northeastern section of Tehran that housed the Tiara Electric Company. He claimed that Project *Magush* had benefited from clandestine Russian, as well as North Korean and Pakistani support. Shirazi himself had worked with North Korean engineers on the design of nuclear-capable missile systems.

This stuff was not within Alberto's official purview, which was to catch terrorists. Maybe he could bump the problem over the *Centro Nacional de Inteligencia*, the CNI, which was heavily populated with military intelligence officers and had a fine analytical section. The Iranian's next words, however, changed everything.

The desperate fear in his eyes was easy to read as he said, *"There are two nuclear devices on Spanish soil."*

The Iranian might as well have said that UFO's had landed at Retiro Park for an alien tour of the Prado because he could offer no proof beyond his words. Alberto, whose profession demanded circumspection, was incredulous. Many experts believed that a nuclear attack somewhere by terrorists was inevitable, and there had been scattered failed attempts to assemble "dirty" bombs. So he was faced with the need to determine whether this Iranian was crazy or whether the fear that plagued the sleep of every counter-terrorist official in the world had just landed on his narrow shoulders?

"You'd better explain that, Major."

Shirazi claimed that a group he knew only as *"La Hermandad"* had purchased the devices some five years earlier from the commander of a former Soviet garrison. The devices had been clandestinely shipped out of a Black Sea port and delivered to the southern Spanish port of Algeciras on an unknown date.

"Back in Tehran such rumors are common,

and all those stories about suitcase bombs were just crazy. But now VEVAK is somehow directly involved because it was they who sent me here. VEVAK has many contacts in many places, especially in the world of contraband nuclear materials. Don't forget how much A.Q. Khan's network helped Iran in its acquisition of centrifuge technology. It is a vast web, and they feel all the vibrations that pass through it."

The Iranian paused to wipe the perspiration from his brow as Alberto stared wordlessly. Alarm klaxons shrieked in his mind – atom bombs in Spain? Could it be true?

"Last summer *La Hermandad* contacted VEVAK via a contact in Morocco and asked for a favor. VEVAK agreed, with the blessings of the Supreme Leader Ayatollah Ali Khameini."

"What favor; and why would VEVAK want to be involved?"

"The Islamic Republic supports many groups and organizations, so long as they promote the spread and eventual victory of Islam."

"*La Hermandad* doesn't sound like an Islamist group," said Alberto. "There are many *Hermandad's* in Spain associated with the Catholic Church. They organize festivals and march on holy days. The original *hermandad* was a sort of medieval police force that existed in Spain centuries ago. They were the predecessors of the *Guardia Civil*."

Shirazi shook his head stubbornly.

"I don't know about that. All I know is that

VEVAK sent me here on a mission."

The Iranian paused again, as though deeply embarrassed.

"Tell me about the mission."

Refusing to meet the Spaniard's eyes, Shirazi said, "When such weapons are stored or transferred the firing mechanisms are disconnected and rendered inert. My task is to make certain they're functional and then arm them to detonate. It's the reason I was sent to Madrid.

CHAPTER 7

The CIA man stopped dead in his tracks to gape at the Spanish cop.

"Believe me," Alberto concluded, "I hope he's lying, but I don't know how much time we have. I'm betting everything that the CIA has the resources to confirm or deny his claim."

"Alberto, you need to take this to your government immediately! We'll do all we can to help, but your own people should know about this." Shirazi had suddenly developed a greenish, radioactive glow.

Alberto had to crane his neck to look into the former football player's face.

"Vop, I just can't do that right now. I need PROOF, concrete facts, before I can pass this to the Moncloa. I can't risk news of it getting out before we have the situation in hand, and I guarantee that as soon as this information is put into the hands of the politicians it'll be only a matter of time before it hits the newspapers. If

Shirazi's claim is true, if he's really on a mission here to set off nuclear bombs, he's the only link we have to this so-called *Hermandad*. Whoever has the weapons will have to contact him sooner or later. Publicity would destroy the advantage Shirazi gives us, and these people would find another way to achieve their goal, a way we won't know anything about. I just can't risk the only lead we have. I'm sorry to put you in this position, but I have no other choice."

The CIA had had its own share of grief thanks to leaks to the press. Operations of enormous importance to US national security had been blown for the sake of headlines and a few days' notoriety. Alberto was right: the Iranian would have to see this through whether he wanted to or not.

They shook hands and parted, and Strachey, his thoughts a jumble, hurried to retrieve his car. The next meeting with Shirazi was set for the day after tomorrow, and Langley had to be informed. He hoped his writing skills were up to the task.

CHAPTER 8

Alberto was exhausted. He dragged himself through the door of his fourth floor apartment and was greeted by the pleasing onion and potato aroma of a *tortilla española*. His promotion had made it possible for him to move his family to a new apartment building in the bedroom community of Las Rosas, just west of Madrid proper. It was not a luxurious apartment (an honest cop could never have afforded luxury), but it was modestly comfortable and boasted two bedrooms.

Elena was in the living room idly staring at the television; ergo it was Anna, his daughter, who was in the kitchen preparing the family's evening meal. This did not surprise Alberto, but it saddened him that his 18-year-old daughter had assumed the role of mother. A pretty, young girl should still be out having fun with her friends at this hour or primping for a date.

"Dinner will be ready in fifteen minutes, Papa," Anna sang from the kitchen. "Just *tortilla* and salad. Is that OK?"

His eyes still on Elena, Alberto answered, "That sounds perfect, *mi hijita*."

He spotted the half-empty glass of vodka on the table beside the sofa and shook his head morosely, his lips compressed tightly. This would never end, he knew. It had been five years now, and each month since the tragedy had etched deep lines on his wife's once beautiful face.

He crossed the small living room, bent over the back of the sofa to kiss Elena on the cheek, resting his hands lightly on her shoulders. "How are you today, my dear?"

"The same," she said, her voice slightly slurred by the vodka. "Are you home already?" She smiled up at him, a smile that seemed to glimmer dimly from some depth Alberto could no longer reach, like a candle flickering in a dark tunnel. This woman, he thought, was once vivacious and a joy to be near, but now was a wraith, here but not here.

"It's past ten, Elena, and Anna almost has dinner ready," he said gently. "Why don't I clear this stuff from the coffee table, and we can all eat in here tonight. There must be something amusing on TV." She squeezed her eyes shut as he retrieved the vodka, and a single tear slid down her cheek.

Alberto was resigned to his wife's permanent fugue, not that he ignored her needs or did not understand and sympathize. His loss was no less than hers, after all. But his nature did not permit external forces to defeat him. He supposed he was fortunate to have a reason to leave the apartment each day, to have a job, a vocation that pleased and fulfilled him – and one that promised a measure of revenge, of justice.

Elena was the archetypical earth mother, a kind, nurturing soul who lived for her children. She would have been happy to have remained in the village on the *meseta* where they had grown up together, Sepúlveda, where Alberto's family had been prosperous merchants for generations. But the tiny village locked in the fastness of Castile and León could not contain Alberto's imagination, and his restlessness had taken them to Madrid, a city that Elena had only ever tolerated. He suspected that she at some level faulted his ambition for the tragedy that had befallen them.

His eyes strayed involuntarily from the wreckage of his wife to the family photos arrayed on a shelf above the television set. It was a spot where they were always in view, and Alberto had considered moving them. One frame, still adorned with black crepe after five years, contained a photograph of their son, David. It showed the young man, still in his teens, in his rugby uniform, long black hair tousled, jubilant in a victory his team had just won. Alberto had taken that photo himself. Next to it was an ancient and battered dagger in a curved brass sheath that had been David's favorite possession as a boy. He had found it one summer while digging through the attic of his grandparent's house in Sepúlveda.

On March 11, 2004, David Macías was returning to the city center from an overnight stay with a friend when two bombs exploded at precisely 7:38 AM when the train he was riding was stopped at the *El Pozo* station. The bombs had been placed in the upper levels of wagons four and five. Sixty-seven people died and another two hundred more were injured. It had been impossible to recover David's entire body.

At the same moment another bomb ripped through a train in *Santa Eugenia* Station killing 17 and injuring 25. Even more devastating, seven other bombs had exploded on two trains at Madrid's huge Atocha station resulting in 136 deaths and 400 injured. In all, the ten bombs that destroyed the trains during the morning commuting hour on March 11, 2004, killed 191 people and left another 1,858 injured. Later investigation determined that all the affected trains had originated at Alcala de Henares, east of Madrid proper.

Alberto knew only too well that hundreds of families besides his own continued to suffer. And despite organized efforts at counseling, despite the prayers and condolences and psychologists thoughtfully provided by the state, there was no real surcease, no "closure." There were only scarred souls that refused to heal completely.

And now he was burdened with the heavy

knowledge that an even deadlier threat loomed over his country. He knew he would not sleep that night.

Shirazi's claim was clearly beyond the capabilities of the CNP to confirm. If it were true, the Iranian could not be permitted to defect because another could be sent in his place and the danger would remain. Without a lead to the people who had the bombs, the so-called *Hermandad*, there would be no chance to prevent a catastrophe. The Iranian's motivation was to escape with his family before something terrible happened. That could not be permitted. Shirazi would have to stay where he was until his story could be sorted out and the bombs found.

The *Comisario Principal* was reluctant to hand the matter up the ladder where it would be agonized over and pummeled by political interests. Shirazi's story would be like the proverbial elephant in a room full of blind men.

His superior, the Director of the National Police, was a Socialist appointee with political rather than police instincts and Alberto believed he was unreliable. Ricardo Sevillano came from a family of wealthy Andalusian aristocrats, and Alberto had instantly disliked him. There was something about the man that left him cold. He couldn't quite put his finger on it, but Alberto had learned to trust his instincts.

In Madrid's pressure cooker atmosphere the story would without doubt be leaked in short order to one of the big newspapers, *El Pais* or *El*

Mundo, or worse still to the right wing *ABC,* and it would become a political football, whether true or not. There would be widespread panic. Precipitate action was out of the question.

He knew it was egotistical, even dangerous for him to believe that he and only he would make the right decisions as the drama progressed toward an unknowable end. But it wouldn't be the first time he had taken matters into his own hands -- one of the reasons he was so effective at what he did.

The terrorist attacks of March 11, 2004, had been the deadliest in Europe since the bombing of Pan Am Flight 103 over Lockerbie, Scotland in 1988. It had been estimated that in monetary terms it had cost the terrorists only some fifty thousand U.S. dollars to execute. Whether it was *Al Qaeda* or the Moroccan Islamic Combatant Group (GICM) to which several of the murderers belonged did not matter to Alberto – so many had died, including his son. He detested all terrorists and the deviant beliefs that inspired them.

CHAPTER 9

As instructed, the Iranian met with them in a room that Alberto had arranged at the venerable but shabby Hotel Cuzco on the *Paseo de Castellana*, the city's main thoroughfare. The roar of traffic reached them faintly through the window from the always busy *Plaza de Cuzco* ten stories below. Alberto sat in a chair at the side while Strachey and Shirazi faced one another over a coffee table, Strachey taking notes while the Iranian nursed a coke.

Shirazi again resisted Strachey's demand that he remain in place, but the CIA man patiently pointed out that Shirazi was a blank page as far as CIA was concerned. The Iranian would have to prove his worth before he and his family could expect to go to the United States.

Shirazi launched an exasperated look in Alberto's direction. "But didn't he tell you what I said?"

Alberto's face remained impassive.

"Why don't you tell me?" asked Strachey.

The Iranian major sighed and recited the story Alberto had detailed to Strachey at their earlier meeting regarding his employment in the Iranian nuclear weapons program. Strachey elicited enough additional detail regarding the identities of co-workers, the location of weapons laboratories, and the overall structure of the program to give Langley's analysts sufficient information to make an initial source evaluation and probably a restricted codeword report directly to the White House. More penetrating questions would eventually be formulated at Langley.

"Now tell me about the nuclear devices you say are in Spain. What kind of 'nuclear devices?'"

"There is a difference between a nuclear 'device,' and a nuclear weapon. Basically, a 'device' is capable of generating a nuclear explosion, but it has not been weaponized, reduced in size to the point where it can be placed in a bomb or a warhead. A 'device,' strictly speaking, can just blow a big hole in the ground wherever it happens to be sitting; it can't be remotely delivered. They are typically quite large. Even the Hiroshima bomb weighed about 8,000 lbs. In this instance we're talking about tactical nuclear weapons, nuclear land mines, actually. They weigh approximately 4,500 kilograms and have a yield of 10 kilotons each."

The thought of the equivalent of 10,000 tons of TNT exploding in the center of any city was horrific.

"Why Spain?" This was a point that genuinely puzzled Strachey. "Were these things sold to ETA?"

The bloodthirsty Basque terrorist organization had in the past developed close ties within the shadowy world of international terrorism. The radical communist Provisional Irish Republican Army was but one example of their enablers. Images of the organized terrorism in Western Europe of the seventies flashed through Strachey's mind. But he doubted that ETA had the kind of connections, let alone the cash, to acquire nuclear weapons. Dynamite and plastique were more their style.

"I don't know, but there must be an Islamist connection of some sort or VEVAK would not be involved and the mullahs would never have agreed."

"You can't identify the buyer? The weapons, the 'devices,' were allegedly delivered several years ago, yet nothing has happened until now. You say your mission in Spain is to arm them, but you don't know when, where, or with whom you are supposed to work. You'll have to do better than that, my friend."

Shirazi was piqued.

"I am to receive instructions when the time comes, just before the operation is to be launched. And it shouldn't be long or I wouldn't have been sent here in the first place." He glared at Strachey. "You're an intelligence officer. Isn't that the way you would do it?"

The Iranian was right. Need to know was basic tradecraft, but the situation was not advancing Alberto's cause. Maybe Langley had some leads to alleged sales of Russian nukes that would match the Iranian's claim.

CHAPTER 10

Firouz Shirazi fought to conceal the panic which had tied his gut in knots when Colonel Aref Zarin strolled unannounced into his office at the Iranian Embassy. The VEVAK officer had shaved his beard, but he was immediately recognizable. It was the morning following his meeting with the Spanish and the American intelligence officer, and his first thought was that he had been discovered. Had VEVAK kept him under surveillance?

The last time he had seen the Colonel was in Tehran when he had been briefed on his assignment to Madrid. On that occasion, Zarin had been in full uniform, seated behind an imposing desk at the tall VEVAK building off of Pasdaran Avenue in north Tehran. But today the blond haired, blue eyed Colonel was in mufti looking like a Northern European tourist. No one would take the handsome blond man for an Iranian.

The bottom fell out of Shirazi's stomach. What was Zarin doing in Spain?

"Salaam Aleikom, Peace be with you, Major," Zarin smiled.

Shirazi bolted out of his chair, almost knocking it over, to stand at attention.

"And with you, Colonel."

A heavy premonition of impending disaster almost buckled his knees.

"Sit, sit back down," said Zarin easily, "We have many things to discuss. The time has come for you to complete your mission." He sat across from Shirazi, comfortably crossing his legs.

Shirazi struggled to regain his composure and blurted, "But the Spanish have not contacted me!"

Zarin smiled indulgently. He appeared to be in a sunny mood that contrasted with the darkness swirling in Shirazi's head.

"No, Major, of course not. They contacted ME. It would have been much too dangerous for them to approach you directly. The line of communications with the *Hermandad* runs through Tehran. I have come to escort you to meet our friends."

"When?"

"Now. I have a car outside."

Shirazi suppressed the scream that bubbled up inside him.

"You seem apprehensive, Major," said Zarin. He chuckled, "But I shouldn't wonder. You will soon strike a mighty blow against the infidels. I shouldn't be surprised, in the fullness of time, if poems were written in your honor. Your brother would be proud." He checked his watch and looked expectantly at Shirazi. "Are you ready?"

"I need to see my wife ... tell her I'll be away for a while. I'll have to pack some clothes."

If he could get away from Zarin for just a moment he would try to slip out of the embassy with his family and get away. It would be a desperate gamble, but he was willing to take it. He started to rise.

Zarin waved a dismissive hand.

"There's no need for that, Major. Your wife already has been notified that you will be absent for a few days, and she packed a bag for you. Our concern right now is to get you out of the embassy safely and take you to our friends so you can get to work. The great event is only days away."

It was devastatingly clear to Shirazi that the VEVAK officer was not going to let him out of his sight.

Zarin stood.

"Shall we go, Major?" He was growing impatient.

Shirazi could do nothing but obey. In the embassy compound's enclosed garage Zarin's rented Mercedes sedan was waiting beside the embassy's official cars and a truck with a covered cargo area that had been parked there for several days. He followed the Colonel's instruction to lie in the back seat with a blanket covering him as they drove out of the compound and turned into

Calle de Jerez.

"Stay down until I tell you."

Zarin drove to *Avenida Pio XII* where he turned south to the traffic circle at *Plaza de la Republica Dominicana* then east, finally merging into the fast moving south bound traffic on the M-30. An hour passed before he was satisfied that no one was following and pulled over to permit Shirazi to join him in the front seat. He saw that they were on the A-5 highway, heading southwest. He had no idea where their destination might lie.

*****

Across the street from the Iranian Embassy José Solís of the UAO, the CNP's *Unidad de Apoyo Operativo*, Operational Support Unit, had observed and photographed the large Mercedes sedan entering the compound. It had left an hour later with the same blond man at the wheel. Solís noted the time and logged the license number then continued his vigil for signs of Firouz Shirazi.

CHAPTER 11

Langley, Virginia

Strachey's report had definitely captured the attention of someone important at Langley. He received instructions to fly to Washington as soon as it hit the desk of Jack Teacher, the Chief of the Counter Terrorism Center.

Strachey's habit was to have a double scotch, eat the airline meal, and fall soundly asleep until just before landing. Headquarters had paid for a Business Class ticket, but even the enhanced accommodation, abundant food, and better quality scotch could not lull him to sleep this time. Fanatics were planning to unleash nuclear fire on an unsuspecting population, and every time he closed his eyes he saw only flames and ashes.

An hour after landing and a tedious drive from Dulles International Airport, he showed his credentials at the Route 123 gate and steered the rental car through the park-like campus of CIA Headquarters, now snow covered, promising a white Christmas in a few days' time. He followed the circular drive to the front of the original Headquarters building to the small VIP parking lot located to the left of the main entrance. He was still stiff from the long flight and there was a persistent throbbing in his head. He was pleasantly surprised that someone in Admin had considered him important enough to merit a VIP parking space thus saving him the long hike in through the slush from the far distant West Parking Lot. He strode up the broad front steps under the cement portico and paused to stamp the snow off his shoes before entering the building.

A statue of Nathan Hale stood to the right of the entrance, head and shoulders draped in snow. It had always struck him as ironic that the Agency so honored a spy who had been captured and hanged because he had practiced poor tradecraft by carrying a secret message hidden in his shoe. Noble intent did not guarantee success. But perhaps it was a sly reminder that we should learn from our failures.

Once past security, Strachey continued through the building past the portraits of past CIA directors until he had entered the New Headquarters Building where he took the elevator down four floors to the sub-level where the CTC had been re-located. The unit originally had been on the DDI side of the old building, which originally housed bespectacled analysts cosseted away from Operations like virginal medieval princesses. Things had changed over the years, and these days the analysts liked to think they were part of operations. Strachey had a Freudian view of this as analytical penis envy.

The CTC 'bat cave' looked like a movie set with its subdued florescent lighting, myriad TV and computer monitors glowing and huge displays on the walls, some of them transmitting live images from CIA drones half a world away. As he navigated through the maze of cubicles he spotted several familiar faces waiting for him behind the glass of the conference room that sat illuminated like an aquarium in the center of the room, and his apprehension jumped a peg. The aquarium was full of sharks, big sharks.

There was the European Division Chief, David Hurley, a slightly built man with a fringe of white hair and the mannerisms of a college professor. Teacher was thick and burly, ready to wrestle the enemy to the mat and make him say uncle. And much to his surprise he recognized the genteel profile of the Deputy Director of National Clandestine Services, Terence Stoddard, impeccably dressed, old school tie, and carefully trimmed moustache. The fourth man was Harvey Grant, the Deputy Director of Intelligence – the Agency's top analyst. Grant's exact age was unknown, but he had been a fixture in the DDI seemingly forever. He had an open face highlighted by stunningly piercing blue eyes behind wire-framed glasses.

Whether such an august reception was a good thing or a bad thing Strachey would find out when he entered the conference room. These were the guys everybody in the Agency sought to emulate, the guys who made the hard decisions.

He shook hands all around and Teacher gruffly invited him to sit at the head of the table to brief the group. All of the men with the exception of Stoddard, were in shirtsleeves, and their expressions were not dissimilar to that of someone who has discovered a fly in their soup. Somewhat self-consciously, he told them the story. Nobody said a word until he was finished. He left nothing out, including Alberto Macías's insistence on being the sole CIA contact.

They all sat quietly for a moment digesting his words until, at a nod from Stoddard, Teacher spoke. "Bob, you've done a great job on this. Your initial report on Shirazi was a stunner. You could have heard a mouse pissing on a cotton ball in China when we read the part about the Russians. He has the potential to be the most significant human source we have ever had on the Iranian nuclear weapons program. I assume you've already figured that one out."

At 5'8" and 220 lbs. no one would have mistaken Jack Teacher for a fashion plate. He always looked a little disheveled, as though he had never learned properly to dress himself. But despite his penchant for ribald humor and his appearance the shock of unkempt brown hair falling across his forehead could not disguise the sharp intelligence that shone from his eyes. A son of Alabama but a graduate of Harvard, he was plain spoken and had been known to fearlessly ruffle high ranking feathers.

Jack Teacher, like the colleagues gathered with him, was a member of the Senior Intelligence Service – the equivalent of a General officer in the military – and he had been dealt a tough hand. The jackals in Congress were in full throated cry to draw and quarter Agency officers who had participated in terrorist interrogations, the Justice Department had launched one of its periodic raids on the Agency, and the FBI was gloating because it looked like terrorism once again was to be treated as a criminal matter. The old walls were being resurrected and feral, weasel-eyed lawyers were closing in from all sides. And yet the thirst for more and better intelligence was unquenchable. Teacher was not demoralized; he was simply royally pissed off most of the time.

He continued, "I'll be frank with you, Bob. We've never had a source that had actually been INSIDE the nuke program over there." He glanced around the table. "But no one is too pleased with this Spanish Police involvement."

Strachey opened his mouth to protest, but Teacher headed him off.

"We know, Bob, we know. Without them we wouldn't have Shirazi in the first place, and we'll be properly grateful for that and live with it. But the Spanish have never been high on our list of allies, and since they pulled out of Iraq they've had even fewer friends around here. In a little while we'd like you to tell us about this Macías fellow, what he's like, what kind of game he's playing."

In sharp contrast to Teacher, the urbane DNCS, Terence Stoddard, cut a spare, elegant figure. He reminded Strachey of an aging, sandy-haired Errol Flynn complete with natty moustache and his hair combed in a style that would have been at home in the 1930's. Stoddard had recently been called out of retirement to take over the National Clandestine Service, an unenviable job at a time when risk-taking had become unfashionable.

"Shirazi's assertions concerning Russian nukes in Spain are, as you might expect, not a little disconcerting. We can't hold onto such information indefinitely without reporting it, even sharing it with the Spanish government, so it's imperative that we determine whether the Iranian is credible. From all appearances, he is. His name appears on a list the Israelis compiled of officials involved in the Iranian nuclear program. They must have acquired the information from a clandestine source inside Iran."

Strachey immediately assumed this was a list of people slated for assassination by the Mossad's *Kidon* unit.

Stoddard was still talking. "We'll still need to box him as soon as possible, but for now his *bona fides* look promising."

Bingo, thought Strachey, but he worried that there might not be enough time to arrange a polygraph before decisions had to be made - tough decisions.

DI Harvey Grant pushed his gold wire framed glasses to the crown of his head, slightly disheveling his thin comb-over, and took over.

"If Shirazi's claim regarding the nukes in Spain is true, the implications are staggering. It's one thing for the Iranians to flaunt their illegal nuclear weapons program under the collective nose of the international community, but it's quite another actually to detonate a nuclear device in Western Europe. If they actually were to do it and their culpability were discovered they would risk devastating retaliation. Shirazi's claims are spectacular, but unverified, perhaps a subterfuge to induce us to accept his defection. But for the moment, let's assume he's telling the truth.

"VEVAK has been caught in the past trying to blow things up in Europe. In 1995 they tried to smuggle a 320mm mortar into Belgium via Antwerp, intended to destroy the offices of an Iranian resistance group in Paris."

Teacher muttered something that sounded like, "Crazy fuckers."

Grant continued, "We're trying to figure out why Spain might be chosen as a target this time. Is it because Spain possesses no nuclear weapons and is otherwise incapable of mounting any serious unilateral retaliatory action? Are the

Iranians crazy enough to ignore the fact that Spain is a member of NATO? And what about the rest of Europe? Is Tehran counting on the Europeans to blink? France is the only Continental nuclear power, and no one would expect the French to launch a nuclear strike unless they were hit themselves.

"Another possibility is that the Iranians are counting on our being able to detect a Russian weapons signature in the aftermath so their hand would remain concealed. Any way you cut it, all hell could break loose, and we could find ourselves with another war on our hands, possibly a nuclear war."

They seemed to be missing the point. Strachey held up a hand to interrupt Grant.

"What you're saying assumes that the alleged nuclear attack is strictly an Iranian operation with Iranian goals in mind. What about the rest of the story? Shirazi says the Russian weapons were acquired illegally, apparently old Soviet tactical nukes, by some sort of Spanish group, and the Iranians are only providing covert technical assistance. Tehran wouldn't expect there to be any connection to them when all is said and done if it's a home grown job."

Teacher folded his arms and leaned back in his chair. He didn't look convinced.

"I wonder," said Grant, "but even so, why Spain? What would anyone have to gain? We're pretty sure ETA isn't up to anything remotely this dangerous, and no one has ever heard of this

Hermandad outfit. It doesn't sound like the Spanish have either. And the Spanish services have done a pretty good job mopping up Al Qaeda types since M-11, haven't they?"

Strachey nodded. "But M-11 did happen. There's no doubt that was an Islamist attack."

"Yes," Teacher replied, "but the Spanish capitulated and pulled their troops out of Iraq."

Grant continued, "Frankly, this Spanish bomb thing is so bizarre that we are forced to treat your source with some circumspection, and that limits the extent to which we should hold his information close. On the other hand, it is so outrageous that we could decide not to disseminate it, at all. It's not outside the realm of possibility that Shirazi is a provocation, especially in light of his claim that the Russians are providing covert assistance to the Iranian nuclear weapons program. This puts us in a real bind."

David Hurley spoke up. "Certainly, there is the possibility that Shirazi's story is just that – a story. But if he is really involved in Iranian nuclear weapons development, as the Israeli information tells us, you can bet there will be strong pressure to turn him and run him as an internal source."

Strachey had expected this, but he had a counter-argument. "For now, at least, that's not an option. If he's telling the truth about the nukes and they are detonated, the CIA's goose would be cooked for good if it came out that we had foreknowledge and did nothing."

"No one is suggesting we do nothing, Bob," rasped Teacher. "But this stopped being a normal case the moment Shirazi mentioned loose nukes and the Iranian program. A decision has to be made, here and now, and it will be. You're the only one who's seen the guy in the flesh, talked with him. What's your impression?"

Strachey was all too conscious of the fact that his answer to this question was what all of these heavyweights had gathered to hear. These were the graybeards of the CIA who had weathered many battles, made good decisions and bad decisions, and bore the scars to prove it. They were wise enough to know that nothing could substitute for the first-hand impressions of a trained case officer.

He chose his words carefully.

"He doesn't FEEL like a provocation. I think he believes what he says. There is very real fear there when he says he wants to be taken out of Spain."

Recalling his conversation with Alberto Macías, Strachey added, "Macías doesn't know what to believe either, but he can't take the chance that it's just a story to justify a defection."

Stoddard asked, "Why didn't Macías take this to his own people? I find his action in coming to us bizarre."

Strachey explained Alberto's fears about leaks to the press and ensuing panic and concluded, "The most important thing for Macías is that Shirazi be kept in place until his story can be sorted out. If his story is true, the devices can't be detonated without him, and he'll be contacted sooner or later. Right now that's the only chance we have of finding the weapons before they're detonated, if they exist."

Teacher interjected, "So Macías doesn't want anything handled through the normal liaison channels on this case? We have to treat this as a unilateral operation, at least for the time being?"

"Up to a point, but Macías insists we share everything we have with him. When the time comes we'll have to rely on him to take the appropriate action. Remember, the CNP are cops, and they can't move without solid evidence, just like the FBI."

But Strachey wondered if the *Comisario Principal* might not act on his own, with or without solid evidence.

Grant, the DI, said, "And neither can we." He turned to Terence Stoddard, his equal in rank as DNCS, "I agree that we shouldn't release this information until we've taken a closer look. At the same time, it's just too explosive, no pun intended, for us to wait indefinitely. Do you agree, Terry?"

Stoddard stroked his moustache. With a sidewise glance at Teacher, he said, "Yes. I agree. But this Spanish cop is right: any leaks and everything turns to shit."

Teacher, who had been burned by politicians before, said, "You're probably right, but as Bob says, if something blows, and I mean blows nuclear, and the White House and the rest find out that we had some advance warning and didn't tell them we might as well put a padlock on the door because we'll all be out of business, if not in prison."

"So our problem is not so different from Alberto's," said Strachey.

Stoddard nodded. "Making certain that the information we provide to policymakers is correct and not passing on every crazy rumor we hear IS our business. But dismissing information that doesn't fit preconceived notions also is unacceptable. That's what happened with that Iranian defector Zakeri in Baku in 2001. He had detailed information on the September 11 attacks, but the jackasses sent to debrief him didn't believe it. That mistake cannot be made again.

"At the other extreme, we took a beating over weapons of mass destruction in Iraq, and we were convinced that that info was solid. WMD in Spain is even more problematic. That makes it all the more urgent that we settle the matter as soon as possible, and given the stakes, 'as soon as possible' means yesterday."

He turned to Strachey. "When do you go back to Madrid?"

"Not later than the day after tomorrow, Terry. Macías and I have another meeting with Shirazi scheduled that afternoon. I arrive in the morning, and the meeting is the same afternoon."

One of the few traditions, at least, of the old

CIA remained: everyone used first names, even with superiors.

"That doesn't leave much time for preparation," said the DI. "I have an idea." He looked around the room. "This is a perfect operation for Palantir. It should give us a leg up."

"What's Palantir," asked Strachey.

"You'll find out soon enough, Bob."

The DI turned to Stoddard. "Terry, I know there's a lot of operational stuff you and Jack want to sort out with Bob, but I'd like to have him for at least half a day tomorrow. I want to put him together with Amy Dawson to get a Palantir program up and running. It could speed the resolution of this thing considerably."

Stoddard shot a glance at Strachey.

"You can sleep on the plane on the way back, Bob. You're not going to get much rest while you're here. The tech people are waiting for you now, and your ops briefings begin at 0700 hours tomorrow. We'll arrange for a polygraph operator to fly to Madrid for the meeting with Shirazi."

CHAPTER 12

Technical Services explained that if they were indeed dealing with a Soviet landmine it was most likely a model developed in the 70's containing a plutonium core surrounded by high explosives. Weighing in at nearly five tons, these weapons had been intended for placement along the Sino-Soviet border where the Russians had long anticipated an invasion. The weapon could be triggered either by an internal timer set by retreating troops or remotely, and the resulting explosion would cause massive destruction and radioactive contamination over a wide area.

In the end the point was that they made big bangs and killed lots of people, both in the immediate blast and later through radiation sickness. The alleged 10 kiloton "yield" of the Russian nuclear land mines would produce a blast only slightly less devastating than the Hiroshima A-bomb.

Strachey managed about four hours' sleep

at his Tyson's Corner hotel before heading back to Langley for the morning ops briefings. David Hurley, the European Division Chief, and Jack Teacher were in charge of these. Strachey suspected that one of their main objectives was to determine whether he was up to job. He couldn't blame them; a lot would depend on the field officer's judgment in this case, and events would accelerate rapidly when and if Shirazi finally was contacted by the terrorists.

Apparently he passed muster.

When the session was nearly over, Hurley unveiled a surprise.

"Bob, how do you and Sidney Jones get along?"

"Fine. Sidney's pretty laid back, but he made the right decision when I briefed him on Shirazi."

By "laid back" they all recognized that Strachey meant "cautious."

"Does Sidney have a good relationship with the Ambassador?" Hurley asked innocently.

This was a loaded question because Ambassador Griffin Palmer, a political appointee who considered himself superior in intellect to most of mankind, was well known for his disdain of the CIA. Sidney Jones had cultivated the Ambassador's trust by assuring him that the Station would never undertake an operation without first clearing it with him. As there had been no real clandestine operations since Jones' arrival in Madrid, no harm was done, and

Ambassador Palmer was a happy camper.

Strachey decided on a diplomatic response to Hurley's question.

"Yes. Sidney's done a good job with Palmer."

Hurley smiled at Strachey's loyal reply.

"We know all about Palmer. With apologies to Jack's *alma* mater, he's a conceited ivory tower academic and political opportunist, and I wouldn't trust him from here to the door. Jack and I think the world of Sidney, but if you have to run everything you do past him, you risk not only slowing things to a crawl, but Sidney might decide he needs to brief the Ambassador, as is his prerogative. If that happens Palmer will find a way to get between us and the Spanish, and he would be an impediment to any action we might have to take."

Hurley and Teacher exchanged meaningful looks.

"Bob, we're going to call Sidney home for 'consultations,'" said Teacher. "We'll make sure he's out of Spain until this thing is settled. He won't mind bringing his family home for Christmas. That means you'll be Acting Chief of Station. Is that ok with you?"

It looked like they trusted him. That was nice, but it also meant that the full weight of decision-making and action would be on his shoulders. If anything went wrong, it would be HIS head on the pike. *Stop thinking like a damned bureaucrat! This is what you joined up for!*

"I guess so, but I'll be working closely with

Alberto Macías."

"That's your call," said Hurley, "just keep that damned Ambassador out of the loop."

Teacher added, "We don't have long, maybe only days, to arrive at some sort of closure on this. The pressure will build quickly to brief the White House. Once that's done, it's going to be out of our hands. Explain that to Macías."

CHAPTER 13

That afternoon Harvey Grant introduced Strachey to Amy Dawson, a petite African-American girl with a *café au lait* complexion and large, intelligent brown eyes. Strachey, chronically unable to penetrate feminine age-defying powers, estimated she could be anywhere between 25 and 35 years old. She wore geeky glasses with black plastic frames and was dressed in a black pant suit over a demur white blouse buttoned up to her neck.

Amy's office was located in a vault deep in the bowels of the New Headquarters Building, protected by an electronic key pad and an iris recognition protocol. Inside was a desk, actually a large work table that was shoved up against a wall upon which hung four huge flat panel display screens. Most of the light in the room came from the screens and a single desk lamp placed to one side of the work table.

Two leather-upholstered executive desk

chairs stood before the work table, and Amy beckoned him to sit down beside her.

"This," she swept her arm toward the displays, "is Palantir."

"Let's start at the beginning. What is Palantir?"

Amy launched into a description she had obviously given many times before. "Basically, it's a search engine, like Google, but an immensely more powerful data mining tool, and what it searches is not the Internet, but the entire U.S. Government security database, which is actually a huge collection of separate databases. There are hundreds of them belonging to the various agencies of government, the military, intelligence, NSA, law enforcement, plus the foreign databases to which we have access.

"Before Palantir, analysts had to search each database separately, manually, and any connections or patterns of activity had to be detected by the individual analyst, usually scratching out his thoughts on a pad of paper. In many ways it was a hit or miss system and a lot of stuff got missed in the past. Another problem was that sometimes a bit of information in a report was classified above the analyst's access. That meant that the entire report was withheld from the analyst.

"Palantir changed all of that. It 'tags' every bit of data separately, for example, so that even if part of a report is classified above the analyst's access, he can still see everything else in the report.

"So this system connects all the dots and sorts all the data. It will even let an analyst know when someone else is working on a similar problem so they can share information and conclusions. Frankly, it's amazing," she concluded proudly.

Strachey was impressed, and his Tarheel sensibilities were delighted to recognize in Amy's voice the unmistakable dulcet intonations of his own North Carolina youth.

"So where do we start?"

"I've already begun," said Amy. "Basically, it works like a Boolean search: you enter a string of key words and wait to see what comes out. It's a little more complicated than that, of course, but you get the idea. I've started with key words like 'Russian nuclear land mines, stolen or sold or missing, Spain, Algeciras, Iran, *Hermandad.*' As we gather more information, we can refine the search further.

"We're actually trying to resolve two riddles at once: is there evidence that the Russians are helping the Iranians develop nuclear weapons, and was a contraband Soviet nuclear device of any sort sold to a Spanish entity? These questions are practically mutually exclusive."

"Yeah," said Strachey, "but for the time being let's just concentrate on the second question. If the source's assertion is true, we don't know how much time we have left before something goes boom in Spain and a city is vaporized along with its inhabitants. And if he's telling the truth about that, his information on the Russians is also likely to be accurate. If we can use him to neutralize the threat in Spain, we can bring him here to be debriefed on the Iranian program." Strachey didn't think there was a way in hell that Shirazi would or even could go back to Tehran as an inside asset.

"I see your point," said Amy. "The claim is that the devices entered Spain several years ago via the port of Algeciras. It's possible that a nuke could have slipped in that way, but only before 2006."

"Why before 2006."

"Because that was the year that we -- actually the Department of Energy's National Nuclear Security Administration -- and the Government of Spain completed installation of radiation detection equipment at that port."

"OK, did your gadget have anything to tell you about missing Soviet nukes?"

She frowned at Strachey's reference to Palantir as a 'gadget' and said, "There's so much information out there on that subject that a year ago it would have been impossible to sort through it all, but thanks to my 'gadget,'" she smiled sweetly at Strachey, "we may have come up with something you can use.

"In late 2003 the NSA intercepted some Russian military communications concerning two nuclear devices, specifically tactical nuclear landmines, which were missing from inventory at a nuclear arms storage site designated Sebezh-5 near the border with Latvia. Six months later we had more intercepts telling us a Twelfth Main Directorate colonel was arrested and executed. The colonel was in charge of one of Rosatom's warhead assembly and disassembly facilities and had a fat numbered bank account in Switzerland. Rosatom is controlled by the Twelfth Main Directorate."

"So, you conclude that the two are related, that the colonel sold the devices?"

"The Twelfth Main Directorate of the Russian General Staff is responsible for the security of nuclear weapons and their storage and maintenance, so this colonel would certainly have had access. But we've not 'concluded' anything yet. We've just begun to interrogate the system."

Having put Strachey in his place, she continued, "We also searched for ships leaving Russian and Latvian ports that off-loaded cargo in Algeciras between 2003 and 2006." She punched a button on her keyboard and a long list poured onto one of the flat screens.

"That's a lot of ships," she said.

"We can narrow that down," said Strachey, "Our source specifically claims that the shipment was made before 2004. The data you have on the missing Soviet devices dates from 2003. Obviously the devices could not have been shipped before they were stolen. So you can narrow down the search to the period following the theft and the end of 2003. That's only a few months."

Amy cocked her head to one side, "If," she said, "if your source is telling the truth."

"That's what we're trying to determine, Amy."

CHAPTER 14

<u>Madrid</u>

Another sleepless flight behind him, the wheels of Strachey's plane touched down on the runway of Barajas International Airport at 7:15 AM and taxied to a Jetway at Terminal 1. With no checked luggage and a diplomatic passport he breezed through Immigration and Customs and emerged into the cavernous reception area ahead of the other passengers. He immediately spotted Alberto Macías making a beeline toward him through the crowd.

The Spanish cop did not look happy. He grabbed Strachey by the elbow and steered him toward the exit where his unmarked car was parked at the curb, lights flashing. Alberto didn't say a word until they had pulled away.

A cold rain was falling again, and the temperature hovered around 40 degrees.

Christmas was two days away.

"We have a problem," were the Spaniard's first words.

"Shirazi?"

"We haven't seen him since you left. I would have called your cell phone before now, but our meeting with him is scheduled for this afternoon. He may just be holed up in the Embassy. I wanted to see if he shows up today before raising the alarm."

"I thought you had round the clock surveillance on him. How did he get away?"

"Our guys can't go inside the embassy. The UAO has an observation post across the street and surveillance teams on call at all times, the phone lines are tapped, and we have coverage of their cell phones, as well. But Shirazi has been completely off the radar for two days."

Alberto studied Strachey as he spoke, wondering if he had been double-crossed, and the American read his thoughts.

"Alberto, the CIA has done nothing with Shirazi, I promise you. In fact, the boys at Headquarters are ready to give you all the support you want."

The reception at Langley had surprised him. Teacher and the others were putting their careers and reputations on the line to protect the integrity of the operation. They were old warriors, and their determination to do the right thing under difficult circumstances had restored a great deal of Strachey's faith in the institution he served.

The Spaniard solemnly nodded, "I believe you, Vop."

This development could spin the operation in an entirely different direction; maybe even end it, leaving an unresolved nuclear question hanging.

"Alberto, can you drop me at my apartment? I want to shower and change into some fresh clothes, and then I have to go to the Embassy. Sidney Jones will be leaving on this afternoon's flight to Washington, and there are some things I have to take care of in the office."

He was disturbed more than he wanted Macías to know, and he needed to get word back to Teacher as soon as possible. If Shirazi didn't show up for this afternoon's meeting decisions would have to be made that were well above Strachey's pay grade. Best if Teacher started thinking about it sooner rather than later. Also, he hoped that Amy Dawson had come up with something they could use.

Macías was curious. "Sidney is leaving? Now?"

"Yes. I'll be Acting COS until this is over."

The always perceptive Alberto gave him a tight smile. "That's good news." He wanted to hear more about Strachey's visit to Washington.

Tired and jet-lagged, the weight of the operation on Strachey's shoulders was almost a physical presence.

CHAPTER 15

Macías and Strachey checked their watches in shared exasperation and disappointment. Christmas now lay only two days in the future. It was nearing four o'clock, and Shirazi was two hours late for their meeting. This time they were at a CNP safehouse under Alberto's control, actually an unoccupied office, not far from the Prado Museum. Their carefully laid plans to track Shirazi to his *Hermandad* contact were falling apart.

The polygraph operator from Frankfurt had been waiting for Strachey at the Station with his equipment packed in an aluminium suitcase, and Macías had not been happy when Strachey arrived at the safehouse with him in tow. The operator now sat by a window looking bored and annoyed by the smoke from Macías's cigarette.

"We have an alternate meeting set for tomorrow," said Strachey hopefully. "Let's not panic yet."

Unable to sit still any longer, Alberto lit another cigarette, stood, and began pacing around the room.

"I have a bad feeling. I don't think he'll show up tomorrow or any other day. I think he's gone. I can FEEL it."

"We have a plan, Alberto, and the plan takes unexpected circumstances into account. That's why we set alternate meeting times."

But no matter how many times you underscored the importance of adherence to the commo plan, as often as not agents did something else.

Strachey felt the same pessimism as his companion, but was unwilling as yet to give in to it. If they could not polygraph Shirazi, Headquarters' reaction was a crap shoot. Personally, he did not consider the polygraph as the *sine qua non* for a decision. The box was useful, but only up to a point. It was not infallible, not even close.

"Let's not give up hope just yet."

He knew that Alberto's mind, just as his own, was filled with a kaleidoscope of horrific images of another M-11, only a thousand times worse. Strachey had briefed him on the missing Russian nuclear land mines, and if the Iranian had escaped their grasp an unimaginable disaster awaited them. Had his instinct failed him? He thought of all the information in Shirazi's head about the Iranian nuclear program, information that would be vital to his government. Should he have accepted Shirazi's defection? No. Their only chance to learn the location of the devices would have been lost. Alberto would have rebelled. People would die.

Macías turned to him. His voice edged with the bitterness, he said, "Hope! We can't count on hope. Our job is to think the worst, and that's what I'm thinking now. If we've lost Shirazi, we may have lost everything."

He resumed pacing, his agitation rising ever closer to the surface.

"If you were one of these Salafist fanatics, what day would you choose for an attack? What is the most sacred day for Christians?"

"Christmas! You think the attack is planned for Christmas."

It was a statement, not a question as the logic struck home.

"Precisely."

"That's only two days from today."

"Yes."

"You think we can't afford to just wait until tomorrow to see if he shows up. What can we do, Alberto?"

"Two things: first, I'm going to get in touch with Nico Villagas and have him place a call to the embassy and ask to speak with Shirazi on the chance that he's still there and just could not get away today; second, I'm going to check the photos and records from the observation post on *Calle de Jerez*. They may have missed something."

Strachey said, "I want to go with you. Any information we uncover should to go to Langley immediately. We might be able to salvage something, even if Shirazi is really gone."

He was thinking of Amy Dawson and Palantir.

A half-hour later they were in Nico Villagas' office listening as he called the Iranian Embassy. Nico wasn't having any luck. He replaced the receiver in its cradle as he shook his head. "No matter what I said they insisted he was 'unavailable.'"

They thanked him and left immediately for the *Calle de Jerez* observation post.

*****

The OP was set up in the front room of a vacant second story apartment facing the Iranian Embassy compound across the street. The walled diplomatic compound was a self-contained unit consisting of a large, L-shaped complex of offices and apartments surrounding a large garden and swimming pool. There was a single vehicular entrance on *Calle de Jerez*.

The UAO operatives were taken by surprise when Alberto introduced the American, but they quickly got over their shock. The two were now poring over the logs and photos of the past few days. There had not been much activity. Diplomatic activities in the Spanish capital were at low ebb in view of the impending Holidays.

Alberto held up a photograph.

"What's this?"

The photo showed a blue Mercedes sedan with non-diplomatic plates entering the compound. The profile of the blond-haired driver was clearly depicted.

José Solís took the proffered photograph and scanned it.

"I remember this. It could have been someone applying for a visa, I suppose. I took the photo because it was unusual for a civilian car to enter the compound. Most visitors park on the street. The same car left about an hour later, and there should be several more photos in the pile, including some taken by one of our men at street level."

Alberto found the other time-stamped photos and the corresponding log entries.

"I'm going to take these, José," said Alberto.

"Sure, *jefe*. No problem. This is your show."

Alberto placed the documents in a folder.

"I'll contact you tomorrow. Be prepared to close this operation down. I may have a new assignment for you and your team."

In the car, Alberto said, "Vop, I'm going to trace this car. It won't take long."

Strachey was still thinking about Palantir.

"I'd like a couple of the photos, especially the ones that show the driver. Can you let me know who the car belongs to as soon as you find out?"

"Pick out the ones you want. I'll drop you at the embassy on the way to my office and call you on your cell as soon as the trace is completed. It won't take long, and I want to see if your people have anything on the driver."

"I'll hold my message to Langley until I hear from you. Be quick."

CHAPTER 16

Colonel Zarin was accustomed to people not being terribly chatty in his presence and didn't mind the lack of conversation during the five hour drive from Madrid. The man beside him was a means to an end, a mere technician who would serve the ends of the Islamic Revolution, just as had his Basij brother – pawns on a chessboard that Zarin controlled. That Shirazi would do what he was told was all Zarin needed to know.

The Mercedes' on-board GPS did its job, and Zarin now turned into a graveled drive and braked before an ornate set of electronically controlled wrought iron gates. A sign announced that they were entering the "*Pasofinos Fernandez*" ranch. There was a call box equipped with a closed circuit television camera at the side of the drive, and a disembodied voice asked their business.

"Please tell Mr. Fernandez that his package

is here," Zarin spoke in accented English.

After a short pause the iron grilled double gates swung open to permit them to enter. The drive was unusually long through a grove of olive trees, and the large, whitewashed adobe hacienda with red tile roof could not be seen from the entrance. When it finally came into view three men were standing in the circular drive in front of the house.

*****

With some difficulty, Shirazi had come to grips with his situation. The Spanish and the CIA had failed him. A man must accept his fate. When Zarin appeared so unexpectedly he had feared that his contact with the enemy had been discovered, but it quickly became clear that the VEVAK colonel's mission was to deliver him to the *Hermandad*, whoever they might be.

The impressive house they were approaching, the well-maintained grounds, and the stand of olive trees on both sides of the drive bespoke great wealth, and Shirazi began to understand that he was not to be delivered into the hands of some ragtag group of sweaty fanatics.

The Mercedes rolled quietly to a stop beside the waiting men. Two of them were obviously guards, and they contrasted sharply with the elegant figure that stood between them.

The man was not particularly imposing

physically, but nevertheless projected an aura of authority and strength. His silver hair was well groomed and swept back from a high, patrician forehead. Shirazi estimated his age at somewhere between 50 and 60. He was dressed casually, but expensively, in corduroy trousers and a light turtleneck sweater.

The Andalusian weather was decidedly warmer than in Madrid, but with the winter sun now sinking toward the horizon, a chill hung in the air.

Shirazi was startled to hear Zarin address one of the guards in Farsi before striding around the car, his arms outstretched toward their host. "Salaam Aleikom, Sultan." Who was this "sultan" who maintained Iranian guards?

The man stepped forward and embraced Zarin, planting a kiss on each cheek.

"It is good to see you again, Colonel Zarin," he said in English, then turned his eyes to Shirazi. "And this is the *baradar* we have been waiting for?" He used the Farsi term for brother.

"Yes," replied Zarin, clapping a hand on Shirazi's shoulder. "This is Major Firouz Shirazi. He is well-trained and prepared for this mission." He addressed Shirazi, "Major, this is our esteemed host, Don Miguel Fernandez."

Shirazi inclined his head deferentially.

"You are familiar with Russian technology, Major?" asked Fernandez.

"Yes, sir, I have been working in that area for several years."

"Excellent," replied the man with a smile. "Your assistance will be critical to our success." He glanced over his shoulder at the setting sun. "It's nearing the hour for the *Maghrib*, my brothers. I'm sure you will wish to join us for evening prayers. Afterwards we can inspect the device."

When prayers commenced Shirazi found it difficult to find the peace and concentration dictated by the Qur'an, and he hoped Allah would forgive the transgression. His discomfort was amplified by the differences between the Shiite and Sunni prayer rituals, from the *Wuduu* ablutions to the form and content of the prayers. He felt as though he had stepped into a parallel universe. By contrast, Zarin was completely at ease.

Afterwards their host led the two Iranians to a large concrete bunker that stood opposite the house where Fernandez unlocked a heavy door and swung it inward. He switched on powerful overhead lights before deactivating an alarm system.

The room, Shirazi noted, was climate controlled and apparently had its own independent emergency power source in the form of a large generator that stood beside the bunker.

A dull gray metal cylinder rested in a custom built cradle and Shirazi could see the worn Cyrillic stenciling on its side:

РС-117 ☢ ОСТОРОЖНО

A large electrical circuit box was mounted on a wall, and a thick cable snaked from across the floor to an umbilical connector on the weapon's side. An identical support cradle stood next to the first, but it was empty.

"Please, Major, I would appreciate your opinion," said Fernandez.

Shirazi stepped to the cylinder's flat end where a heavy access hatch had been opened. The device was about five feet in diameter and ten feet in length, and Shirazi knew it weighed nearly five tons. Grabbing a flashlight from a worktable nearby upon which also lay the heavy access hatch cover, he peered inside. He knew the device was over two decades old, but despite the worn appearance of the outer shell, the interior was pristine.

The device had been deactivated for shipment and storage by removing the power supply from the trigger and disconnecting the trigger itself from the weapon's internal circuits. The diodes on the control panel that monitored the condition of the explosive charge, the core, and the electrical circuitry burned steadily as he checked the digital readouts beside them.

"Do you find it to be in order?" asked Fernandez, and for the first time Shirazi detected a note of anxiety in his voice.

When he hesitated, Zarin moved quickly to his side, and he could feel the cold blue eyes boring into his back.

"I think so," he said. "The control panel

indicates that the core material remains viable, and the system is within operational parameters, but I am unsure of the status of the internal power supply. It may have degenerated over the years."

"Yes, yes, I know that," said Fernandez. "We will use an external back-up power supply for the operation. But otherwise, do you believe it's functional?"

"All that is required is to connect the arming device in the proper sequence, program it with the activation code, and set the timer." Shirazi was chilled by his own words.

"And you can do this, Major?" asked Fernandez.

With a quick glance over his shoulder at Zarin, Shirazi replied, "Yes, sir, assuming you have the activation code."

"I do. And how long will it take to complete the arming sequence?"

"No longer than five to ten minutes."

"Excellent," breathed Fernandez, and his face suffused in a smile.

*****

They shared a simple meal that evening in the extravagant dining room during which Fernandez briefed them on his plan. Zarin listened raptly as Fernandez described his vision for a revenant *Al Andaluz*, but the more Shirazi heard, the more convinced he became that these were the ravings of a lunatic.

Was it possible that Zarin was so benumbed by his own fanaticism that he could not recognize the utter implausibility of Fernandez's vision? Or was something else going on? Was Iran supporting this monstrous plot for the sake of sowing chaos in the West, without regard for the consequences?

Shirazi had long ago concluded that his country's president, who reminded him of a rabid chimpanzee, was dangerously unstable, and the mullahs were no different. Did they really expect the Spanish Government and the Europeans just to surrender a huge swath of territory to a gang of criminal terrorists? And what would the United States or Israel do should the Iranian hand be revealed in the murder of tens of thousands of people? He was in the hands of madmen.

"As for the targets," their host continued contentedly, "Madrid is, of course, the most likely, but it is important that we preserve the Government of Spain so that a formal and legal devolution of *Al Andaluz* is possible.

"First, we will destroy a different, less important Spanish city so that they will know they are dealing with serious people. After that we will issue our ultimatum – accede to our demands or Madrid will be next. They will not dare to refuse us."

They retired to the sumptuously furnished living room, and the Iranians' discerning eyes noted with appreciation the fine Persian carpets

MICHAEL R. DAVIDSON

that covered the tiled floor. Shirazi thought he recognized the rich earth tones of at least two authentic Fereghan Sarouks.

"Please sit with me over here near the fire."

Fernandez took a seat in front of a huge field stone fireplace in which firewood had been laid on a bed of dried grape vines tied into bundles. There were several leather covered armchairs ranged around the hearth.

Fernandez's butler/bodyguard entered carrying a tray with a recharged coffee service that he placed on one of the occasional tables before kneeling to light the fire, which blazed up immediately warming the faces of Fernandez and his guests.

"Did you know," Fernandez asked, "that grape vines make the best kindling."

Soon the logs had caught and were blazing steadily, casting a faux cheeriness over the room.

Lifting the exquisite silver pot, Fernandez poured the rich, dark liquid into their cups, the gesture of a gracious host. He turned to Shirazi, who had barely spoken a word.

"And you, Major Shirazi, shall ignite the fire that will change the world. You shall have my everlasting gratitude."

He beamed as though he were offering Shirazi a precious gift.

Zarin, who had listened quietly as he sipped his coffee, asked, "Are you satisfied with your security, Sultan?"

Fernandez's smile was confident.

"We have influence in the government in Madrid, even in the security services. I assure you, everything that happens in Madrid is known to me."

The blood in Shirazi's veins turned to ice.

CHAPTER 17

That night Shirazi's sleep was disturbed by the same dreams and memories that had plagued him since his youth.

In the dream his brother, fifteen year old Majid, could clearly see the tip of the landmine's black prong protruding from the swirling sand just a few yards, a few more steps, in front of him, and his hand rose involuntarily to the plastic key that dangled from a cord around his neck. All around him the broad expanse that separated the Iranian trenches from the Iraqi line was festooned with sudden eruptions of sand that rose high into the air, like red-tinged flowers, where other mines had exploded under the feet of his fellow Basij.

But the mine a few steps ahead was Majid's mine and his alone. The terrible din of battle faded now as he imagined himself rising on silvery clouds to eternal glory and honor, and he felt nothing but ecstasy as he brought his foot confidently down on the prong.

Majid belonged to the Ayatollah Khomeini's Basij Mostazafan, *or "mobilization of the oppressed." Each* Basij *wore a crimson scarf tied around his neck and some had been issued old rifles or hand grenades to hurl at the enemy who waited across no man's land and would attempt to repel them with tanks, rockets, and machineguns.*

At the appointed hour, with the sun rising at their backs, the Basij *climbed over the lips of the trenches, organized themselves into straight ranks as they had been trained and charged fearlessly into the withering fire from the Iraqi lines in wave after wave while behind them the better armed and trained Revolutionary Guard and regular army troops waited for the mines to be cleared.*

One day in 1985 two strange imams had appeared in their poor village and assembled the entire population of 150 in the main plaza. The Ayatollah Khomeini needed soldiers for God and each family in the village with children was ordered to provide one son who would martyr himself to open the way for the arrival of the Twelfth Imam, the "Mahdi." The invasion of the apostate Iraqis, they said, was a "gift from Heaven." The imams showed the villagers some trinkets in the form of plastic keys that they promised would open the gates of Heaven for the martyrs. (The Ayatollah Khomeini had purchased a large shipment of these cheap plastic trinkets from a manufacturer in Taiwan.)

The Shirazi family had two sons, Majid who

was fifteen, and Firouz who was eight. Their father was the village mechanic and blacksmith, an important position. Their education was rudimentary, limited to learning passages from the Qur'an by rote, and both boys spent most of their time learning their father's trade in his small machine shop. The words of the strange imams had inspired both boys, but Firouz was too young (12 was the minimum age), and so it had been Majid who was chosen to go, despite the tearful protestations of their mother, Ghamzeh.

Majid had marched proudly from the village, grinning broadly as he waved good-bye.

In his nightmare Firouz was unable to turn away as his brother's foot touched the mine causing the propelling charge in its base to ignite and launch it up out of the sand until it reached a height of about 18 inches when its tether wire released a plunger that set off the mine's charge, firing deadly fragments of steel in a lethal circle that raggedly sliced Majid's legs from his body and sent hot shrapnel through his organs. Instead of being transported instantaneously to Paradise, Majid lay on his back staring uncomprehendingly at a sky smudged darkly by the smoke of war, the shredded stumps of his legs spurting gouts of arterial blood that soaked immediately into the hot, dry sand. In a very few moments the sharp fingers of pain scratched through the thin skein of shock into his brain and he screamed for his mother as he bled to death.

Shirazi awoke drenched in sweat, stifling

his own scream in his pillow.

CHAPTER 18

<u>Madrid</u>

The deadline for decision was on a collision course with Alberto Macías's habitual caution. The first tendrils of suspicion that the target date was Christmas had taken firm root.

The Holiday would fall on Friday this year. Festive lights were draped along the *Paseo de la Castellana* and all over the Spanish capital, shops thronged with Holiday shoppers, and the huge department store *El Corte Inglés* at *Cuatro Caminos* was doing a thriving business. Between Christmas and New Year's Day, no one would be working throughout Spain. Families would gather at home, go to parties, and visit with relatives -- unaware of the dark radioactive menace that threatened to snuff out the joy of the Season.

A police trace of the license quickly determined that the Mercedes belonged to the

Hertz rental agency at Barajas Airport where it had been rented to a French national, named Guy Parmentier the same day it had appeared at the Iranian Embassy. Parmentier had arrived on the morning Air France flight from Paris. The rental agent identified the blond man in the surveillance photo as the same person who had rented the car.

He immediately shared this information with Strachey to run through the CIA database. The American had promised results by morning, and Alberto now waited impatiently in his office for his arrival.

The *Comisario Principal* had been at his desk since early morning following a nearly sleepless night, and his first action had been to issue an all-points bulletin for the rented Mercedes and to place the Frenchman on a border crossing watchlist. That was all he could do for now, and there was no certainty anyway that the Frenchman had anything at all to do with Shirazi.

If the CIA database yielded nothing and if Shirazi failed to show at today's meeting, Alberto would have to warn the government. A warning could be bolstered by the CIA intelligence that Russian nuclear devices were missing and confirmation of Shirazi's identity, but he could not be certain of the response. Despite Spanish mistrust of the Americans, he would need backing from the CIA. If the warning came from Washington rather than from him, he hoped, the government might take it seriously.

Just after eight A.M. the subaltern in his

outer office informed him that the CIA man had arrived.

Strachey entered carrying a large manila envelope in one hand. The strain that showed on his face signaled that his night had been no more restful than Alberto's. He could only imagine what was going on in Washington.

"I have news," said Strachey as he sank into a chair and stretched his legs. "I don't know if you'll think it's good or bad, but it does tell us something important."

He explained that he had been on the secure line with Amy Dawson and DI Harvey Grant until well after midnight. Without Palantir, days rather than hours would have been required to scan the multitude of scattered databases, and even then, putting the clues together would have been hit or miss, subject to human error.

Alberto leaned forward on his elbows, intent on what Strachey might have found out and impatient for him to get to the point. David had been sitting on that train at the *El Pozo* station in March 2004. He had surely been chatting with his friends, anticipating what they would do that day, expecting to do many things in the lives that stretched before them. But the bombs had robbed them of those lives. Had they known in that instant between the explosion and its impact what was happening? Had there been time for fear? What did "instantaneous death" mean? Did such immediate annihilation now lay in wait, ticking in some vile metal tube, for thousands more?

The American tossed the envelope on the desk between them.

"That's the full report, but I'll summarize. The man who rented the car is not French. His travel documents were forged. We were able to identify him thanks to the photos from your observation post. He's a VEVAK colonel named Aref Zarin, the very officer Shirazi told us recruited him. You'd never guess he was Iranian with that blond hair and blue eyes, but believe it or not there are still lots of descendants of Alexander the Great in Iran, and a blond Iranian is not as rare as you might think."

The CIA's Palantir had performed remarkably well. Strachey explained that the facial recognition technology built into the system had required less than one hour to match the Spanish surveillance photos to cached photos known to be of Zarin. The Iranian's counterfeit French passport information gleaned from the Hertz rental contract had been checked against a French database that contained all issued French passports.

"Zarin has appeared on our screens before," Strachey continued. "He's been seen at a couple of international conferences, and he has travelled to North Korea with Iranian delegations. We've notified the French to be on the lookout for him if he tries to return to Iran through France."

Alberto opened his mouth to protest, but Strachey forestalled him.

"Don't worry. All we told them was that he's believed to have recently transited France on the way to Spain and may be returning to Iran via the same route, nothing more."

"Where does this information leave us?" wondered Alberto out loud. "VEVAK involvement lends weight to the story Shirazi told. He was expecting contact from this *Hermandad* group here in Spain. This could mean that the contact was via Tehran, which would have been more secure. Your information makes it even more likely that Shirazi left the embassy in that car with Zarin."

"I agree," said Strachey. "What do you want to do now?"

Alberto filled him in on the actions he had taken earlier in the morning. "With luck the *Guardia Civil* might intercept Zarin if he's still on the road, but he could have driven anywhere in Spain by now."

"Yeah, it's the proverbial needle in a haystack."

Alberto kneaded his knuckles into his burning eyes.

"I'm convinced that they intend to do this thing on Christmas Day. That leaves us almost no time. The devices could already be in place in the target cities waiting only for Shirazi to arm them." His eyes strayed to the window. "One of which is probably Madrid."

Strachey followed Alberto's gaze. "One 15 kiloton atom bomb wiped out Hiroshima," he said.

"These nuclear land mines are considered tactical nuclear devices, but some are as powerful as the Hiroshima and Nagasaki bombs."

They had to make a decision, go into action.

"I don't think we can wait any longer to notify the Government. With this new information only a fool could fail to take notice, although without Shirazi I can't say what can really be done besides hunker down and wait for the attack. We have his statements, your confirmation of the missing Russian weapons, and now his disappearance combined with the arrival of a senior VEVAK operative. We just don't know where they are."

"There's something else," said Strachey. "It's not much, and it's in the report, but Langley did confirm the arrival in the Port of Algeciras of ships that had previously transited Russian and Latvian ports during the period we suspect the devices were delivered. There's not much trade between Russia and Spain even today and there was even less at the time. Still, there's a list of the ships here that your people can check out."

"There's not enough time."

Alberto's voice was grim as he shook his head. The strain and fatigue were taking their toll.

"There's not enough time between now and Christmas to wait for results. We've got to act now."

Strachey agreed.

"If only we could locate Shirazi. He's the

key, both for us and for the terrorists."

"And to locate Shirazi we need to locate Zarin."

"It's still early in the day," said Strachey. "If by some miracle Shirazi turns up at the alternate meeting today we can breathe a little easier."

"We'll both be dead of nervous exhaustion if we just sit around waiting for him to show, and we both know he won't," insisted Alberto. "Would Langley be willing to issue an official terrorist threat alert on this so it looks like the information originated there?"

"I'm pretty sure Langley is itching to do just that. But an alert isn't going to force your government to take action."

"Perhaps not, but with no Shirazi and no guarantee we can prevent an attack, at least the Government will be warned. If the threat alert is strong enough, perhaps they'll be convinced and lives could be saved."

The American chewed his lip. "They may do nothing, you know, not even mobilize emergency reaction units, least of all over a big holiday week-end. They could gamble that it's an empty threat, like so many others, so they will want to avoid the absolute panic a public announcement would cause. Otherwise, every security resource in the country would have to be called into play to handle it, including the military."

Alberto agreed to a certain extent, but he could no longer justify keeping his government in the dark. His original plan lay in ruins: he had lost his primary source and the only lead to the perpetrators.

He had often contemplated the ironies of intelligence work which was so different from straight police work for which his training had prepared him. If one reported an apparently substantiated threat that did not materialize, any subsequent such report would be viewed askance, if not with outright derision, as the American CIA had learned in the case of Iraq. In any event, the consumers of intelligence, the politicians, viewed everything through the lens of their own political interests, and one could never know quite what to expect from them.

The value of secrecy was another conundrum he had discovered as head of the CNP's intelligence operations. It was a powerful weapon if wielded with care, but it could come back to bite you, too. It was always a delicate balancing act – what to tell the politicians and when. Because once a secret was released from the safety of the operational world, it was lost forever, and with it went control. It was for that reason that intelligence operators guarded them so jealously.

But how could he continue to keep secret the threat of an impending nuclear attack on a Spanish city? Was there any sort of moral justification for not disclosing it now? Was there even a thread of a chance of foiling the terrorist plot? If not, would the political class be prepared to incite widespread panic throughout the country at the height of the Holiday season?

The answer – probably not, and everyone would sit with their thumbs up their asses and their eyes closed hoping nothing would happen, and if it did, there were always the intelligence services to blame – and the Americans.

CHAPTER 19

Langley, Virginia

It was three o'clock in the morning, and Amy Dawson still sat slumped before her glowing screens. She wanted a cigarette badly, yearning for a hit of nicotine but refused to surrender to her urges and remained immobile, deep in thought. Palantir had given all it could and now the process had been transferred to Amy's very human brain.

CIA Headquarters was deserted at this hour, except for the ops room upstairs, CTC, and the Communications Center. The silence that had settled over the huge building was comforting, a rare privilege to be one of the guardians of the nation who "never slept."

There was something at the very edge of her consciousness, something in the Spanish data that hinted at a resolution. She felt this, but it refused to bubble to the surface. Therefore she sat, reviewed the Palantir readouts yet again, and waited for whatever it was to gel in her mind.

At 3:30 AM it happened. The car! The blue Mercedes rented by the VEVAK colonel. That was it.

She calculated that it must already be 9:30 A.M. in Madrid and dialed Strachey's cell phone.

*****

They were still debating the next step when Strachey's phone beeped in his pocket. He immediately recognized the CIA number, thumbed the receive button, and put the phone to his ear.

Amy Dawson's voice reached him through the ether.

"Bob, it's Amy. I know this is not a secure line, but I figured you would be with the Spanish police, and I didn't think this could wait." A short pause for breath, "Bob, I think I have a way to find the guy you're looking for."

"I'm listening. Don't worry about the secure line. You're right. We're running out of time."

Amy's voice was breathless with excitement.

"The car, Bob, the rental car is the key."

"Sure it is, Amy. We just don't know where it is."

"But we can find it. According to the rental company records it's a late model Mercedes, high end, with an integral GPS system. These high end models all have theft protection associated with the GPS, as well as a separate tracking device. That means it can be tracked and located!"

"You're kidding."

Despite her fatigue, Amy giggled.

"Now, would I kid you, Bob?"

"So, what do we do? Just go to Hertz and ask them to locate it?"

"Probably as simple as that. GPS isn't a complicated system to use. This car might also be equipped with a form of Lo-Jack or something similar as part of the original equipment package. Lo-Jack operates differently than GPS – a small unit in the car broadcasts a radio signal that when remotely activated can be picked up by special receivers in aircraft or police cars. There's a company in Spain called Detector that operates the system. They've been around since 2000."

Strachey lowered his cell phone and grinned at Alberto.

"We're idiots. The rental car had GPS!"

Alberto slapped his forehead. Fatigue had muddled his thinking.

"Of course, it might be possible to track Zarin' car remotely."

He grabbed his coat from the rack and was heading out the door before Strachey could rise from his seat.

"I'll get back to you, Amy," he said as he chased after Alberto, "You're an angel!"

*****

At Langley, Amy Dawson beamed at the compliment. She replaced the receiver in its cradle and stretched her arms over her head. The tension that had kept her thoughts in motion disappeared, and the lack of sleep overtook her as she began shutting down the Palantir system. Twenty minutes later she was in her pink Volkswagen Beetle with the wilted rose in the flower holder heading for her one-bedroom garden apartment in near-by McLean. Despite the freezing pre-dawn air, she had the window down and was puffing furiously on a Salem, counting on it to keep her awake until she could fall into bed.

CHAPTER 20

Madrid

The main offices of Hertz were located at the Plaza de España, a short distance from Alberto's *Calle de Leganitos* office, and that was where the two headed first. Alberto's credentials ensured that they received all the cooperation they needed, and the office staff confirmed that all their premium rental cars were equipped with GPS locators, as well as Lo-Jack. Strachey silently praised Amy Dawson simultaneously kicking himself for not having come up with it on his own.

The office manager led them to a room containing several computers and introduced them to the company's chief of security, an ex-cop who bore the unusual alliterative name of Godofredo Gonzalez. Everyone called him Fredo. Having matched the Mercedes' rental contract with the company file on the car, Fredo sat at a computer console and typed in some numbers. The screen glowed to life with a map of Spain as Alberto and Strachey watched impatiently.

After a few moments, when no blinking dot appeared on the map, Fredo said, "There's no active location indicator, which means that the car is either out of range, which should not be possible, or the signal is blocked. Of course, it's also possible that the system has been disconnected."

"Would turning the unit off disable the search and recovery system?" asked Alberto.

"No, of course not," Fredo replied, "It wouldn't be of much use if that's all it took, would it?"

Fredo obviously took some pride in his position as chief of security. He looked over his shoulder at the two visitors and said with a wicked grin, "This was just the first step, now I'll show you what this system can really do."

He typed some more code into the computer, and a map of Madrid and its environs appeared on the screen, a bright dot was blinking at the location of Barajas International Airport, where the Mercedes had been rented. Slowly at first, but with gathering speed, a wide purple line snaked out of the airport, weaving it's way over the main thoroughfares into the city leading to *Calle de Jerez*. The line continued, heading now for the M-30, the map expanding as the line raced away from Madrid and onto the A-5 highway towards Extremadura. Within two minutes the line ended a few kilometers outside the Sevillian village of Aznalcazar.

Fredo turned toward them again, "As you can see, the system automatically records where the car has been and stores the information even though we can't verify its present location."

Pointing to the screen he said, "That's where the signal ends, and I'll bet the car is still there in a garage or under some sort of roof. You can confirm its location with the Lo-Jack unit, if you wish, but that requires air support."

Strachey asked, "What's there, where the track ends, I wonder. Can you get the coordinates and pull up Google Earth?"

"Sure."

In a few moments they were looking at a bird's eye view of the red tiled roof of a large hacienda that was surrounded by outbuildings and a grove of olive trees.

Fredo punched a few more keys and the printer spewed out a color copy of the image from the screen, complete with map coordinates.

"That's for you, and I'll give you a data sheet with all the vehicle information, including the Mercedes' LoJack frequency."

Back in their car, Alberto called Gordi on his cell phone and instructed him to meet them at the *Calle de Leganitos* office as soon as possible.

Strachey was encouraged by the progress they had made.

"I have to get back to my office and a secure line. I'm going to request satellite coverage of that ranch."

Alberto nodded.

"And I have another request. Ask your people to issue the alert as soon as possible."

"Are you sure you still want the alert issued?"

"Yes. We have so little time left and no guarantees. At the very least the emergency services people might be prepared. I'm going to order a U.E.D.E. unit dispatched immediately to the area along with a GEO detachment."

This was the *Unidad Especial Deactivado de Explosivos*, or TEDAX, the CNP unit responsible for explosive ordnance disposal, including chemical, biological, and nuclear weapons.

"They'll have radiological detection gear. If the devices are on that property, they'll find them."

They had entered the acceleration phase of the operation. Issuing an alert at this time was prudent and unlikely to interfere with the operational steps they were setting in motion.

"I agree," said Strachey. "I'll meet you back at your office in time to go to the safehouse."

Despite their conviction that Shirazi would not appear, the planned meeting still had to be covered.

*****

Strachey closed his officer door, grabbed the secure phone and dialed Teacher's number. It was six A.M. in Washington, but he knew that Teacher was usually in by 5:30. In fact, the CTC Chief had spent the night in his office.

Teacher's voice came on the line, slightly distorted by the encryption.

"Jack, it's Bob Strachey. Things are breaking fast here. In a few minutes I'll be sending you an Eyes Only message containing the coordinates of where we believe Zarin and Shirazi went to ground. You can thank Amy Dawson, by the way, for figuring out how to do it." The young Palantir analyst deserved a lot of credit. "Do you think you can get KH-11 coverage on the site?"

Teacher was silent for a few seconds, and Strachey could picture him calculating the odds.

"I can make a priority override request to NRO for it."

The National Reconnaissance Office rather than the CIA was now in charge of satellite imagery for the U.S. Government.

"How fast we can lock onto your site depends on where the satellite is in orbit right now. The military will complain if we pull one of them away from battlefield coverage in Afghanistan."

"Yeah, I hate to do it, too, but the possibility of a nuclear strike in Western Europe should take precedence."

Strachey heard Teacher yelling for someone to come into his office pronto.

"And, Jack, there's another thing. I want you to ask the DI to issue a terrorism alert to the

Spanish Government right away. Tell him to include as much detail as possible, but ask him not to mention Alberto Macías or Firouz Shirazi. He can give them everything on Zarin's arrival in Spain, though."

"We'll just say it came from an 'Iranian source.' That should protect Macías and Shirazi," said Teacher.

Strachey was surprised by the quick agreement, but then Teacher added, "Bob, we've been busy here. Despite the lack of a polygraph we felt the preponderance of the evidence justifies action. We briefed in the DCI and then all of us, Stoddard, Grant, the DCI, and I went to the White House to brief the President and the national security advisor. It was not an easy meeting. That snake of a national security advisor said she was reminded of Tenant's "slam dunk" briefing to Bush about WMD in Iraq, and that Bush had launched an unnecessary war because of it. It's one of the few times I've seen Terry Stoddard angry. He pointed out that if Tenant's mistake had launched a war, we were trying to do the opposite – stop one before it got started. He also warned that it was inevitable that it would leak to the press that the President knew about an impending attack on a NATO country and did nothing about it. It was a close-run thing, but we have White House backing now, and that sets a lot of wheels in motion. No one asked, so we didn't mention we still lack a polygraph."

Strachey couldn't think of an adequate

response to that. If this turned out to be a boondoggle, they would all be looking for new jobs. He said, "I don't think Alberto is thinking about protecting himself, Jack. He just thinks his government is more likely to take a warning from Washington seriously. In the meantime, we're moving into high gear here, and with any luck we'll have the bad guys and their bombs wrapped up by tomorrow."

"We damn well better have something wrapped up tomorrow. What else can we do to support you?"

"I'm going to be out of pocket until further notice. I'm going after these guys with Macías, if he'll permit it, and I'm sure he will. I'll take the station's secure satphone with me, and I'll have the cell if all else fails. We'll see if Shirazi shows at the meeting site early this afternoon. I'm sure he won't, but we can't afford to guess wrong. We won't hang around too long, though, if I know Alberto. As soon as you get any KH-11 imagery on line, let me know, OK?"

"OK, Bob, it's your show. I'll get things moving at this end. Stay in touch."

Strachey severed the connection, grabbed the satphone and raced back downstairs to his car. He would link up with Alberto at *Calle de Leganitos*.

CHAPTER 21

Gordi was waiting for Alberto in his office when the *Comisario Principal* returned. In fact, he was reclining in Alberto's chair with his feet propped up on the *Comisario's* desk.

"Damn it, Gordi, you're going to destroy every chair in my office before you're finished."

"I just wanted to see what the seat of power felt like."

Gordi dropped his feet to the floor and stood, gesturing obsequiously at the chair he had just vacated.

"Please," he said with a delicate flourish of his hand.

Ordinarily Alberto would have joined his friend in some light badinage, but now he was all business. Moving behind his desk he impatiently waved Gordi to take the seat opposite.

"Take out your notebook. There's a lot you're going to have to remember."

He spent fifteen minutes bringing his friend up to date.

Gordi was stunned into unaccustomed silence when Alberto described the nuclear threat and his belief that Christmas, now just one day away, was the target date.

"So here's what I want you to do," said Alberto. "Pull your Seville Brigade off holiday leave and order them immediately to find out who owns that property. It looked like a *finca*, a ranch, to me, and it was very extensive. Whoever owns it is wealthy and therefore well-known. Then alert the GEO that I want their best team standing by for orders. Tell them they'll have to commandeer one of the military's Chinook helicopters because a TEDAX team will be travelling with them. If anyone complains about having to call people back from holiday leave, you have my permission to scream loudly at them.

"When you're satisfied that the situation is in hand, go home and pack your bags. We'll meet at the airport at the crack of dawn to fly south," he glanced at his watch, "I'll expect the first report from your local people by then."

Normally he would have commandeered one of the CNP's EC-120 Eurocopters for the flight to Seville, but its range and speed were insufficient for the 820 kilometer journey. He would have to contact the Air Force and request a plane. Going through those channels would take the rest of his day.

*****

Rather than waste time on what he was certain was a lost cause Alberto sent one of his men to the Prado safehouse in case Shirazi turned up. He gave instructions to be notified the minute the Iranian appeared, but he knew it wasn't going to happen.

It was nearing one P.M. when Strachey arrived and Alberto briefed him on his plans.

"I'm going with you, Alberto."

The *Comisario Principal* could have prevented Strachey from joining them if he wished. The involvement of an American in whatever events transpired in Andalusia would be difficult to explain, especially if things went belly up. But the American's help had proven vital, and he deserved to be in at the end.

Strachey said, "I've requested surveillance satellite coverage of the area, and that will give us real time feedback of what's going on at that ranch. You'll need me."

Alberto was impressed. Normally it took the Americans weeks to approve a request for imagery.

"Don't worry, Vop. I wouldn't think of leaving you behind."

CHAPTER 22

Madrid, Christmas Eve Morning

Alberto Macías's plans to fly to Seville were forestalled by a call on his cell phone from CNP Director Ricardo Sevillano at four o'clock in the morning on Christmas Eve.

"Macías, something's come up and I need you at my office immediately."

"Director, I was just leaving to attend to a very important matter."

"Nothing could be more important than what I need to see you about," was Sevillano's curt response.

"Drop whatever you're doing and get over here. And wear a good suit. You're going with me to the Moncloa this morning."

Alberto was just at the point of leaving his apartment for the airport. Chagrined, he turned on his heel and re-entered to change his clothes.

The Director's mention of the presidential palace could mean only one thing – the terrorist alert from Washington had been issued.

The timing could not have been worse, but he had no choice but to heed Sevillano's order.

The drive took only thirty minutes through the deserted streets of the capital at this early hour on the day before Christmas, and when he arrived at the Ministry of Interior building on *Calle de Amador de los Rios* he spotted the heavy, dark haired figure of Sevillano pacing nervously at the main entrance beside a black limousine whose driver had the motor running.

"Get in, Macías, we're leaving right away."

Sevillano was obviously out of sorts, but whether it was from being awakened at such an ungodly hour on Christmas Eve or something else, Alberto couldn't divine. He sat in the rear of the official car with the CNP Director and they sped out of the center of town toward the Moncloa compound at the northwestern edge of the city.

"What's this about?"

The uncommunicative Director shrugged.

"I don't know. The Moncloa called and told me to find you and get there as quickly as possible." He turned in the seat and eyed Alberto suspiciously. "What the hell have you been up to, Macías? Why did they order that you be present?"

"I can't imagine why they should want to see me," lied Alberto as he struggled to contain his frustration.

They rode the rest of the way in silence.

Alberto's suspicions were confirmed when they pulled off of the A-6 highway to enter the Moncloa compound and he spotted the armored Cadillac Deville that belonged to American Ambassador Griffin Palmer and another car with diplomatic license plates. He wondered if Strachey was there, as well.

A uniformed porter ushered them into a first floor conference room off the main corridor. The room was large with several doors that might have led to serving areas or offices. Three crystal chandeliers provided ample light. High backed chairs upholstered in red velvet lined the walls, and in the center was a burnished walnut conference table that could easily have seated forty. But only one end of the table was now occupied.

Alberto was relieved to see Strachey already seated there. The CIA man shot him a look that said 'don't worry and keep quiet' and nodded slightly.

Seated at the head of table was the freshly shaven Spanish President, Julio Camisero, dressed casually in slacks and a starched blue shirt with no tie, the Minister of the Interior, and the Secretary of State for Security. None of them looked happy to be there.

Across from them were the Americans: Ambassador Palmer, Strachey and a bespectacled man with a bad comb-over wearing a wrinkled suit whom Alberto did not recognize.

No one rose to greet them. The President

impatiently waved them to be seated. There were two large carafes of hot coffee on the table and a fine china cup and saucer had been set out at each place next to leather bound note pads bearing the presidential seal, and ball point pens. Alberto could see that Sevillano was vexed to have been the last to arrive.

President Camisero, a slight, spindly man with straight, carefully coiffed black hair and a pencil neck who might have been mistaken for a tax collector, said, "Shall we get started, gentlemen?"

With a sidelong glance at Alberto the President asked Sevillano, "This is *Comisario Principal* Macías?"

"Yes, *Señor Presidente.*"

"Good, then we are all here." Camisero turned toward the Americans. "Well, Ambassador Palmer, what is so urgent that this extraordinary meeting was called the day before Christmas?"

The President of Spain had been awakened an hour earlier by a call from the President of the United States who had informed him that the American Ambassador and the CIA Acting Chief of Station required an immediate audience on a grave matter of national security.

Ambassador Griffin Palmer also had received such a call from the Secretary of State, and he was an unhappy man. Not bothering to hide his pique, he said he had not been informed of the reason but had been instructed to confirm the meeting at the Moncloa Palace and coordinate with Acting Chief of Station Strachey. The CIA man was to meet an incoming U.S. military flight at Barajas Airport bearing the Director for Intelligence of the CIA, Harvey Grant, who would brief the President of Spain.

His resentment still on display and with nothing else to say, Palmer could only introduce the DDI.

"Mr. President, this is Harvey Grant of the Central Intelligence Agency who has been sent to brief us."

The Ambassador settled back in his seat, a petulant expression dragging his face downwards.

Grant extracted a file folder from his briefcase and placed it before him on the table.

"Gentlemen, unfortunately, I do not speak Spanish, and I will ask my colleague, Mr. Strachey, to clarify any points that may not be clear. I apologize for the inconvenience.

"Mr. President, gentlemen, there is no easy way to say this, but we have information indicating that a heretofore unknown terrorist group is planning to detonate a nuclear device somewhere in Spain."

There were gasps of disbelief and alarm from the men around the table. Only Strachey and Alberto remained silent.

Grant continued, his voice calm and firm, "This matter is so serious that we decided that a personal briefing should be provided in lieu of a normal alert notice. I ask you to understand that what I am about to tell you is new information from a new, but credible source." He shot a look at Alberto. "And it appears that your own intelligence services may have supporting information."

The high-level Spanish security officials looked uncomprehendingly from one to the other before all their eyes locked on *Comisario Principal* Alberto Macías who was staring resolutely into his untouched coffee cup.

"Macías, what's this about?" A scowling Sevillano hissed, but was silenced by Grant.

"We'll get to that in a moment, but right now it's important that you understand that the information we have been able to piece together suggests that one and perhaps two ten-kiloton Soviet tactical nuclear landmines arrived in the Port of Algeciras sometime between June and November 2003. We can confirm with a high level of confidence that two such devices were indeed stolen from a nuclear storage facility in Russia during that same period and that several ships sailing from ports accessible to those responsible called at Algeciras during the same period. We are culling through the consignment information for those shipments, but I'm certain you would have easier access to such data.

"Our source, an Iranian official, alleges that one of his countrymen, a specialist, was sent recently to Spain on a mission to arm the devices. We have good reason to believe, therefore, that the target date for detonation is near, and we hypothesize that that date is Christmas day, now only one day away."

The Spanish President, inexperienced in such matters, looked horrified.

"You mentioned an unknown terrorist group. Is there anything else? Do you mean ETA or Al Qaeda?"

Grant's face was grave.

"No, sir. We've never heard of this group before. All the source knew was that it was called the *Hermandad.*"

The Minister of the Interior was incredulous.

"There are many *Hermandad's*, brotherhoods, in Spain. But these are only religious associations that participate in annual festivals. This makes no sense. What is your proof?"

The men around the table nodded, and Ambassador Palmer appeared to be in the grip of acute embarrassment. *Once again,* he thought, *the blundering fools at the Central Intelligence Agency were stirring the pot with lunatic theories. These were the same people who had guaranteed that there were weapons of mass destruction in Iraq! Spain was Palmer's turf as plenipotentiary, and these intelligence people might well leave his tenure in tatters thanks to their antics.* His ire rose along with the voices at the table. His incredulity matched that of the Spanish.

"President Camisero," he said, turning to the head of the table, "I am in the same position as you. This is the first time I have heard any of this, even though it should have been cleared by me before any of you gentlemen were bothered. I can assure you ..."

Harvey Grant had dealt with political appointees of Palmer's stripe for longer than he cared to remember, but he had no time for diplomatic niceties now. He wished that just for once a U.S. Administration would permit the State Department to name professionals to ambassadorial posts rather than pimp them to political hangers-on and wealthy campaign contributors.

Addressing Palmer directly, he said, "Mr. Ambassador, I am here on the personal orders of the President of the United States. If I recall correctly, he considerably outranks you, and HE felt the matter serious enough to request this meeting. If you feel unable to deal with it, you are free to leave at any time. Your presence at this meeting is entirely superfluous, and you were included only as a courtesy."

Palmer's face turned beet red and he started to retort, but apparently thought better of it and clamped his jaws tightly shut.

Grant's words had an immediate effect on the other men present, as well, and they sat in stone faced silence, waiting for him to continue.

With another hard look in the Ambassador's direction, Grant said, "You in Spain have had your own painful experience with terrorist attacks, perhaps more than most Western countries. In the United States we learned our lessons the hard way. If 9/11 taught us anything it was that if it can be imagined, if the wherewithal is available to terrorists, then possibilities that were inconceivable in the past must now be taken seriously. Before 9/11, had terrorists used airplanes? Yes. Had they used explosives? Yes. Had they shown any regard for innocents? No. We KNEW that all the pieces were there for terrorists to fly airplanes into buildings. Some elements of our security services had even identified the terrorists and the fact that they were taking flight training. It was all there for us to see, but we failed. And the consequence of our failure was the loss of 3,000 lives. We learned a hard lesson that day: if you think it could happen, be prepared for it.

"Our Department of Homeland Security is responsible for the National Response Framework, a comprehensive plan for surviving any attack on the United States ... for surviving the unthinkable. That plan lists fifteen possible attack scenarios, and number one is a nuclear attack on a major city. Such a catastrophe would kill tens of thousands of people and the material costs to infrastructure would be in the hundreds of billions of dollars. The resulting chaos would require that martial law be declared. Detailed response planning exists, but even so the idea of coping with such a disaster is daunting. There would be massive evacuations from population centers because everyone would suspect there was a second or third device. Medical facilities would be overwhelmed – in fact, in all the United States there is insufficient medical personnel and equipment to cope with even a single nuclear attack."

Grant had their undivided attention now. He surveyed the somber faces around the table.

"Gentlemen, I may fairly ask: what plans do you have for such a contingency here? Have you thought the unthinkable?"

Ignoring the question, Camisero asked, "Mr. Grant, you said the devices you suspect could be in Spain have a ten kiloton yield. Isn't that very small compared to the thermonuclear warheads on your missiles? These are supposed to be only landmines, after all."

Grant shook his head slowly.

"Mr. President, the atom bomb that destroyed Hiroshima had a yield of only fifteen kilotons."

Then speaking to the group at large, he said, "We take these matters seriously and we felt it imperative that we share whatever information we have that could help prevent an unprecedented disaster here in Spain. That's why we're here."

Grant turned to Strachey.

"Our representative in Spain, Mr. Strachey, only recently brought to our attention supplementary information that could have a direct bearing on this matter. Bob, would you please fill everyone in?"

CHAPTER 23

Strachey had collected Grant at the airport, and the two had rehearsed this part on the way to the meeting in order to protect Macías from any repercussions.

Feeling the heat of Ambassador Palmer's glare, Strachey cleared his throat and took a quick sip of his now tepid, black coffee before beginning. His hand shook slightly as he replaced the cup in its saucer.

"A few days ago, *Comisario* Macías and I were comparing notes on Iranian activities in Spain. The *Comisario*, as part of his counter-terrorist duties, keeps a close eye on all potential threats. Fortunately, *Comisario* Macías had posted surveillance on the Iranian Embassy, and we learned that an unusual individual had visited there the day before yesterday. The *Comisario* had photos of the visitor which he asked me to check against our indices."

Macías's face remained impassive as he listened. The Americans were doing their best to protect him.

Grant passed photos around the table as Strachey continued his narrative.

"We identified the man in the photos as Colonel Aref Zarin, a well-known member of Iran's security and intelligence service, VEVAK. He arrived in Spain on a false French passport. We have good reason to believe that he left the Embassy with the Air Attaché, Major Firouz Shirazi, who has been identified as having worked in Iran's nuclear weapons program. They haven't been seen since.

"When we put this information together with the information concerning the nuclear devices we concluded that there was sufficient cause to issue an alert.

"*Comisario* Macías was able to trace the car driven by Zarin to a rental company and discover that there was a way to find it. He was able to track it to a large estate near Seville, and it apparently has not left the area."

Grant passed some large photos that bore numerous code word security markings around the table.

He said, "These are reconnaissance satellite photos of the place. It's just outside the village of Aznalcazar in Seville Province."

Director Sevillano was looking through slitted eyes at Alberto.

"Is this true, Macías? Why was I not

informed?"

Strachey hurriedly interjected.

"*Comisario* Macías knew nothing about the nuclear report. We've just put this together at Langley."

"Well, *Comisario*," asked Sevillano, obviously annoyed, "What do you have to say about all this?"

Among other talents, Alberto Macías was an expert at the most popular card game in Spain, "*Mus*," a game that depends almost entirely on verbal bluffing, and that skill paid off now.

"Sr. Strachey is correct," he began. "We tracked the Iranians to what I believe is a ranch near Aznalcazar, near Seville. I've already instructed the Provincial Brigade to begin gathering information on the owner. That information should be available later this morning. When the Director called," he nodded toward Sevillano, "I was on my way to Seville to supervise the investigation. What we have heard from our CIA colleagues makes it imperative that I leave immediately and that GEO be called in."

He did not say that he had already alerted the paramilitary force.

"Anything else?" asked the President.

"I also believe we should call in the TEDAX-NRBQ." Alberto referred to the CNP's explosives detection and deactivation unit (U.E.D.E.) that specialized in nuclear, radiological, biological, and chemical weapons disposal.

"If the devices are at the *finca*, they should

be able to find them."

President Camisero, completely out of his depth, looked around the table searching the faces of his senior security personnel. "Do you agree?"

Sevillano spoke up first.   "No, I most emphatically do NOT agree."

CHAPTER 24

He'd known that Sevillano would be piqued, but the man's vehemence nonetheless startled Alberto.

The CNP Director continued, "These gentlemen," and here he indicated the Americans on the other side of the table with a broad sweep of his hand, "are no doubt well-intentioned, but in the final analysis what is it they really have?"

He enumerated his points with his fingers.

"One, they have a barely substantiated report from an unknown Iranian source (or so they say); two, they have information that the Russians lost some nuclear devices several years ago (we've been hearing such rumors for years); three, a man traveling on a French passport whom they CLAIM is actually an Iranian paid a visit to the Iranian Embassy here in Madrid and then drove to the south of the country; and finally, these 'devices' allegedly entered Spain several years ago! If they have been here in the hands of terrorists for so long, why haven't they been used before now? It's illogical."

Sevillano then pointed at Alberto, "And THIS man has been working with the CIA, but for some reason I have received no report from him whatsoever before this meeting."

He gave Alberto a hard look.

"That, *Comisario Principal*, I find frankly disturbing, just as I find disturbing your sudden desire to set matters in motion so quickly this morning without consulting any of your superiors. What do you have to say for yourself, Macías?"

Alberto's gorge rose at the Director's words, and he felt the momentum won by Grant's presentation beginning to slip away.

"Sir," he said, struggling to control his voice. "The urgency is due to the fact that tomorrow is Christmas."

"And what of it?" asked Sevillano. "You and your friends have presented no evidence that supports a contention that Christmas Day is some sort of target date."

"It's the most logical ..."

Sevillano held out peremptory a hand, palm forward, to silence him.

"Logic would seem to have little to do with this entire affair. Take, for example, the allegation that one of the religious fraternities intends to detonate a bomb – ridiculous on the face of it. As I see it, what we have here is a rush to judgment based on very weak and questionable circumstantial evidence."

Casting a withering look at the Americans, he continued, "This is not the first time our American friends have done so."

The President and the other officials in the room had followed this exchange carefully. These were men accustomed to listening to others they considered their peers rather than to subordinates, who were meant to take orders. And the CIA was not held in high esteem by men whose political instincts veered sharply to the Left. Sevillano's argument was having an effect, and it was not to DI Harvey Grant's liking.

"Gentlemen," he interjected forcefully, "I can understand your skepticism, but you simply cannot ignore the threat we have described. At the very least, you should take immediate steps to isolate that ranch until the matter can be sorted out. It's the only lead we have at present to the possible location of the nuclear devices."

Ambassador Palmer saw an opening and took it.

"Mr. President," he said, turning to the head of the table, "as I see it, Director Sevillano's analysis is sound. There have been hundreds of reports since the fall of the Soviet Union that nuclear materials were missing or in the hands of terrorists, and none have been true."

Palmer shot a smug look at Grant.

"I don't think Director Sevillano is advocating 'ignoring' this 'warning.' I think he is saying that it should be handled with circumspection and given such attention as the Government of Spain decides it merits. I'm sure that is what the President of the United States intended by requesting this meeting."

Harvey Grant knew of at least a dozen past warnings that had, in fact, actually prevented the delivery of contraband nuclear materials into the hands of terrorists. He was all too familiar with the pettiness and lack of discipline of political appointees, as well as their penchant for identifying with the host country. He massaged his temples in consternation, trying to think of a way to regain the momentum his presentation had initially achieved.

Before he could speak, Sevillano, taking advantage of Palmer's interjection, seized the moment.

"Ambassador Palmer offers wise counsel, gentlemen," he nodded approvingly at the Ambassador, "and we should take it to heart. We, of course, do take such warnings seriously, given our own long and unfortunate experience with terrorism in this country. We have fought the predations of ETA for many years, and we fought back after the M-11 massacre. We have foiled one terrorist plot after another thanks to improvements we made to our intelligence and counter-terrorist cadres. Why should we expect that we would be less successful in this instance through the application of established methodology?"

Alberto pushed his chair back and stood,

RETRIBUTION

attracting everyone's immediate attention.

Looking like a man about to face a firing squad, he began, his voice halting at first but gathering force as he proceeded. ""*Señores*, the original source of this information is Major Firouz Shirazi, military attaché at the Iranian Embassy. He provided this information to me personally just a few days ago in exchange for assistance in his defection and claimed that he had been sent to Spain for the express purpose of assisting in the detonation of the nuclear devices. I was, of course, shocked, but," and here he looked at Sevillano who was seated beside him, "as the Director just said, I believed more information had to be developed that would confirm or deny the Iranian's claim before bringing it to the attention of the Government. It was for this reason that I turned to the CIA, and within a short amount of time substantiating evidence was uncovered that made the claim entirely credible. The appearance of the VEVAK colonel and the simultaneous disappearance of Shirazi are all the more alarming because Shirazi is the key, and he must be found at all costs before the country is faced with a disaster from which we may never recover. I beg you, gentlemen, allow me to do my duty."

His impromptu peroration finished, Alberto sat down as Strachey and Grant waited breathlessly to see the result.

It was not long in coming.

Sevillano was instantly livid.

"Macías, you called in the Americans

151

without consulting with me, or any other superior? This was a matter clearly of Spanish national concern that could have and SHOULD have been handled within proper channels before seeking FOREIGN assistance. You see now that your thoughtless actions and lack of discipline, surprising in an officer so senior, has led to this international tempest in a teapot. You may consider yourself relieved of duty as of this moment!"

Alberto had taken his best shot and failed. He bowed his head, his face an inscrutable mask.

The President broke the silence that had fallen over the room. Turning to the Americans, he said smoothly, "We thank you for your efforts, and please convey to your president my personal best wishes and gratitude for his interest and generous offer of assistance."

He raked Alberto with a scathing glance before speaking to his senior security officials.

"I agree with Director Sevillano regarding how this matter is to be handled. Please coordinate your activities," and here the President's eyes again focused on Alberto, "and report the results directly to me."

Addressing the Americans again, he continued, "I see nothing more that we can do at this point in time. You surely realize that a public warning regarding such a questionable report would risk widespread panic, and the Holidays further complicate our situation and the investigation. Director Sevillano will take up the matter in due course, and I assure you that it will be investigated thoroughly - by our own people. Thank you again, gentlemen."

The President stood and left the room, and the others followed suit, the Americans exiting ahead of their hosts.

Outside in the drive, Ambassador Palmer approached Strachey and Grant, every inch of his slight, Ivy League frame emanating smug satisfaction.

"Well," he said, "you can be certain the President and Secretary of State will hear of this ridiculous escapade. You have embarrassed the United States, and I assure you that your Director will be properly upbraided for such a lack of judgment."

Addressing Strachey directly, he said, "The next time, if there is a next time, I expect you to pass all such matters through ME before anything is sent to Washington. I am the senior representative of the United States in this country, appointed by the President, and you WILL do things MY way!"

Grant sensed that Strachey's Tarheel temperature had risen to a dangerous level. Despite the temptation to see just how far Palmer might fly if an uppercut were to connect squarely with his narrow jaw, he placed a restraining hand on Strachey's elbow.

He stepped between them and faced Palmer. The two of them were cut from the same physical mold – slight, balding, intellectual – in a word,

ACADEMICS – and they had almost identical backgrounds and education, yet their views of the world and their places in it were completely dissimilar. Whereas the world of the Ambassador was centered entirely on himself and his prerogatives, Grant saw the world as a vast web of relationships and conflicting interests, a dark and dangerous jungle in which his personal needs had long ago been supplanted by a desire serve his country as part of a team of unparalleled professionals. Palmer lived in an imaginary bubble; Grant lived in the real world.

"Ambassador Palmer," he said in a soft but firm voice, his face inches from the diplomat's, "your attitude and actions today, your shocking lack of discipline and abject failure to remember that you represent a government and not just your petty personal interests may well result in a catastrophe of unimaginable proportions that will change the world we live in, and for the worst. In short, Mr. Ambassador, you are a consummate ass. Make sure you include that in your report."

Leaving Palmer red-faced and gasping for breath, Grant turned on his heel, grabbed Strachey by the elbow and pulled him toward their car that sat waiting on the other side of the drive.

Alberto Macías was leaning against the rear bumper, his arms folded, smoking a cigarette.

The Spaniard grinned ruefully and said in halting English, "I'm afraid I'm forced to ask you for a lift into town. I came here with Sevillano, and my car is still parked at the Ministry."

Grant studied him for a moment. "I'm pleased you're still here, *Comisario*. Hop in. We have things to discuss."

CHAPTER 25

CNP Director Ricardo Sevillano, in the rear of his official limousine, pushed the button that raised the sound proof plastic barrier separating him from the driver. He then extracted a non-traceable throw-away cell phone from his inside pocket and dialed a number that was answered after a few rings.

"Sultan," said Sevillano, keeping his voice low regardless of the sound proofing, "we have a serious problem." He outlined for his interlocutor, Miguel Fernandez, what had just transpired at the Moncloa meeting. "I suggest you move quickly and ensure that the Iranians get far away from Aznalcazar. The Spanish authorities will move slowly, but I don't know what the Americans might decide to do. They seemed quite serious. I suggest the Iranians leave the rental car where it is and use other transportation. In another day, it will no longer matter, providing that Shirazi can be induced to cooperate."

When the conversation was finished he replaced the phone in his pocket, sat back in the seat, and let out a long sigh. He had bought the time the *Hermandad* needed to achieve its end. The Sultan had been wise to encourage him to become involved in politics and to seek this position.

He lowered the barrier and instructed the driver to drop him at his home. His wife and children would be packing for their long-planned departure today on "Christmas Vacation." They would be traveling in a first class compartment on the fast train from Madrid to Seville.

*****

In Strachey's car heading back into Madrid proper, Grant was thinking out loud, "Bob, I'm just an analyst. We're going to have to rely on you to make the operational decisions. But whatever we decide," he looked meaningfully at Alberto Macías, "we must decide quickly."

Strachey felt as though he were in some sort of fast-forward dream mode. There's not a case officer alive who hasn't fantasized that the fate of a nation was in his hands and the Headquarters brass were counting on him. It was a nice dream, but the reality was terrifying. What COULD he do under these circumstances?

In a voice that seemed wistful to Strachey, Grant said, "If only Jack Teacher had come instead of me ... But everyone insisted I had the power to persuade other people."

"They don't know the Spanish," said Strachey drily.

"Teacher was the most insistent. He said he would only get in the way, that there was room for only one operational chief in the field, and you knew the turf much better than he." Grant broke out of his reverie. "OK, Bob, what now?"

Strachey decided to toss the ball.

"Alberto, is there anything you can think of that we can do?"

Macías's English, though mediocre, was sufficient for him to have understood the gist of Strachey's exchange with Grant, an exchange that made it clear that he still had a powerful ally.

"Suspended or not," he said, "I've got to get to Seville. What I can accomplish once I'm there in the time we have left, I have no idea, but we can't just let things spiral out of control."

Strachey translated for Grant, who said, "He's right. If the Spanish refuse to take immediate and decisive action, it's up to us."

By "us" Strachey knew he meant the Central Intelligence Agency. "Will Alberto work with us?"

Again, Macías understood. *"Por supuesto,* of course," he said to Strachey. "Right now we have to figure out the logistics."

As an afterthought, he added, "And we'll need some help." He had an idea. "Let's go directly to my office."

Strachey hung a fast U-turn at an

intersection on *Calle de los Reyes Católicos* and headed back for *Calle de la Princesa* that would set them on a direct route back through the *Plaza de España* to Alberto's office. Alberto awakened a grumpy Gordi Castañeda with a second cell phone call and gave him instructions to meet at his office immediately.

"Immediately? What about breakfast?" He was serious.

"Damn it, Gordi, I'll try to have *churros y chocolate* prepared for you at the office. Just get there ... NOW!"

Next he called Nicolas Villagas at home.

When the man's sleepy voice finally came on the line, he said, "Nico, I need your help. Do you still have your jet?" This plane, a Learjet 45, was Nico's latest, favorite toy.

"Of course," replied the airline president.

"Can you have it ready in a couple of hours to fly me and some other people to Seville?"

"Now? At this hour? What's up?"

"I can't tell you on the phone, but things could get a little dicey. I'm working on something dangerous, and I don't have time to go through channels. I need your help."

This was music to Nico's ears, and he came fully awake.

"*Joder*, fuck, Alberto, I'll fly you myself!"

Alberto clapped the cell phone closed and turned to the Americans.

"We have transportation."

CHAPTER 26

<u>Aznalcazar</u>

"Get up and get dressed," the VEVAK colonel's voice held none of its former oily condescension but was harsh with urgency as he roughly shook Shirazi awake. "We have to leave."

Shirazi swung his feet to the floor and tried to rub the sleep from his eyes. Zarin was fully dressed in khaki slacks and a green polo shirt.

"Get dressed," repeated the Colonel, "and pack your things. We're leaving in fifteen minutes!"

Shirazi was startled. *Could this get any worse? What now?*

"Why the change in plans?" he asked as he rose to his feet.

Zarin' hostility could not be mistaken. He wore a disgusted look as he replied, "You should know, Major."

Shirazi's heart skipped a beat. *They know about my contact with the Americans and the Spanish? But how could this be?*

"I don't understand," ventured Shirazi weakly.

"It's too late for more lies," spat Zarin, real anger now giving his voice an even sharper edge. "Your shameful behavior has been revealed to us. There is nothing we do not know."

Is this some sort of test? Are they testing my loyalty?

"What are you talking about?" If he had been discovered he would at least make them say so, see if any deniability remained.

Zarin drew a pistol from behind his back and pointed it at Shirazi. "You are a traitor. You betrayed our plans to the Americans and the Spanish, and now they have tracked us to this place."

So there may be a chance that I will be rescued, but the colonel easily read his thoughts. "Don't get your hopes up, dog. The investigation has been held up by the Sultan's man in Madrid. The cavalry isn't on the way to save the day."

He waved the pistol at the pile of clothes that lay beside Shirazi's bed. "Now, get dressed. We're leaving."

"You're going to kill me." The comment was matter of fact, spoken in a resigned voice. It had been Allah's will that his attempt to escape his fate had failed.

"No, Shirazi, I'm not going to kill you ... yet.

It is an unfortunate fact that we still need your skills to arm the weapons. So you are going with me to the first site, and you will follow my orders."

Shirazi gave up all attempts at pretense. "Are you mad? I will not be responsible for the deaths of thousands of innocent people. I am not a murderer."

"Really," said Zarin, a small, menacing sneer drawing one corner of his mouth upward. "What do you think our nuclear weapons program is for? You had no compunctions about working on that, and you were pleased with the increased salary and the nice things you could buy for your family in Tehran."

Shirazi did not move. If they were going to kill him, then they would have to do it here, in that mad man's fine house.

His voice dripping with disdain Zarin again said, "Now, get dressed. That is the third time I've had to tell you, and I won't do it again. I'll simply call those two large men who work for the Sultan and ask them to dress you."

When Shirazi still did not obey, Zarin said nastily, "You have a fine family, don't you Major - a nice, pretty wife and two lovely children? I would hate to see them end their days in the cells of Evin Prison, and I can swear to you that their ends would not come quickly."

The colonel's cruel words had the desired effect. Shirazi's face contorted in pain and tears suddenly started down his cheeks, but he pulled his clothes on, resigned to his fate.

An expert at manipulating the helpless, Zarin continued, "If our mission is successful, Major, you will still die, but your end will be hailed as a martyr's death like your brother's, and your family will live in comfort and honor in Tehran for the rest of their days. So you see, even to a traitor the Revolution can show mercy and even generosity." It was important to give the man something positive to hold onto. It would make him easier to handle.

The sun had been not long above the horizon when they emerged from the house onto the front drive. Shirazi saw a white Spanish-manufactured Ebro truck with a covered cargo area sitting there with the motor idling. He had the fleeting impression that he had seen the truck before.

Miguel Fernandez waited for them beside the truck observing their approach with sad eyes that Shirazi could not meet. "I am disappointed in you, Major Shirazi, but more serious is the fact that you have disappointed God, ignored his will, and ignored the words of the Prophet, Blessed be His Name. But you are fortunate in that unlike many others who have practiced deception, you are to be given a chance to atone for your sins. God is merciful. Now, go and fulfill your destiny."

Fernandez stood aside as Zarin bundled Shirazi into the passenger seat of the truck's cab. When he had done so, the colonel and Fernandez embraced and exchanged brotherly kisses before the Zarin climbed in behind the wheel.

"May the blessings of God be with you," Fernandez said as they drove away. Within minutes they would enter Spain's excellent network of modern highways and follow a route that would take them and their deadly cargo almost directly north for over 700 kilometers, almost to the Bay of Biscay. Unbeknownst to Shirazi, an identical truck had left the farm some days before, also heading north, but to a different destination.

CHAPTER 27

Strachey's watch told him it was nearing eight A.M. when he, Alberto, and Grant crowded into Alberto's tiny office. A theatrically yawning Gordi arrived fifteen minutes later.

Alberto quickly briefed Gordi on what had transpired at the Moncloa meeting. "*Dios mío,* Alberto, it's worse than we imagined! How could they be so obtuse?"

"That's a rhetorical question, I assume," said Alberto drily, "they're all politicians and above all politicians fear looking foolish."

Strachey said, "It's what we call whistling past the graveyard – if you ignore the possibility of danger, maybe nothing bad will happen."

Harvey Grant, exhausted from his long flight the night before and his fruitless efforts to energize the Spanish President, collapsed onto a chair in the corner of the room. He waved Strachey over to him.

"Bob, if Macías is right about a Christmas attack, we have only hours left to act. Does anybody have a plan?"

"Alberto's trying to organize something, but it looks like he's making it up as he goes along."

Strachey added, "I want to be involved in whatever goes down here, Harvey. It's the kind of thing we were meant to do, and Alberto will have no support from his own people."

Grant smiled wearily up at him.

"Son, you're exactly right. This IS the sort of thing the CIA was created to do. You don't know how much Jack Teacher wanted to make this trip with me. He's a real pit bull, you know. But he decided against it, and I told you why. "As Jack put it, 'There's only room for one rooster in the henhouse.' You're our man on the ground here, Bob, and you're in charge. I'm just an analyst, but I can assure you that, whatever happens, the people you met back at Langley have your back."

Grant could see the impact his words had on Strachey. Like many field officers, the younger man must be unhappy with the increasingly cumbersome bureaucracy and the risk-averse attitude of some senior Agency people. He and the others had carefully reviewed Strachey's record and assessed his personality during their meetings at Headquarters. They'd liked what they'd seen enough to place their own careers in Strachey's hands.

Grant looked up and said, "Tell me what

you want me to do, Bob."

"We'll need someone to keep Langley in the loop, especially if the shit hits the fan. Can you fly down to Seville with us and set up a command post? All we have is a sat phone, but it'll have to do."

Grant chuckled softly. In his entire 30 years with the CIA, this was the first time the sixty-year-old DI had been a part of a real field operation.

"We can do better than that. Teacher sent a bag of tricks along with me that should be useful. The stuff is still at the airport aboard the plane that brought me. And to answer your question, it would be my honor to go with you to Seville."

Grant's exhaustion disappeared and he wondered if the adrenaline levels of field operatives was always as high as his was right now.

Strachey stepped over to where Alberto was briefing Gordi.

"Alberto, you're not going to Seville without us, you know."

Grant watched as Alberto opened a drawer in his desk, removed a holstered pistol, and passed it to Strachey.

"You might need this."

Strachey pulled the weapon from its leather holster, checked to see that a round was chambered and the magazine full, and clipped the holster to his belt.

Alberto tossed him an extra magazine.

It was a Heckler & Koch USP Compact, a relatively light, German pistol that carried thirteen rounds in the clip plus one in the chamber. "That's the CNP's new regulation sidearm," he said, "but I still prefer the old one."

Alberto lifted his jacket to reveal the Star 28PK at his waist.

"I still carry this one. It holds more bullets."

Gordi, who had observed the exchange ran a critical eye over Strachey and asked, "Do you know how to use that?"

"We're not all desk jockeys in the CIA, Gordi, and I was shooting guns practically before I could spell my name. Are you coming with us?"

"I wouldn't miss it." Shifting his gaze to Alberto, he said, "It'll be lots better than *churros y chocolate.*"

"What's the plan?" Grant asked.

"Play it by ear." Precisely the response Grant had expected.

"Just the kind of plan I like best," commented Gordi.

This was definitely not the kind of plan the CIA preferred because it was no plan at all.

*****

Alberto and the saturnine Galician had known one another since they entered the ranks of the CNP together a couple of decades earlier. Loyalty is a strong Spanish trait, and if one makes a friend of a Spaniard, one has a friend for life, no matter what. Gordi had to know full well that his career would be finished if he joined Alberto's enterprise. This, Strachey reflected, was the full measure of true friendship. But courage and friendship would not suffice if they encountered determined opposition.

Striding to the door Alberto said, "We have to get to the airport. Nico will be waiting for us."

*****

An hour later Strachey, Grant, Alberto, and Gordi reclined in the Lear Jet's comfortable seats as Nico's plane accelerated down the runway at Barajas International Airport. In the aisle between them sat two large, black duffel bags containing the gear Jack Teacher had sent with Grant, including a sophisticated radiation detector and two P-90 submachine guns with ten 50-round magazines each filled with special SS190 ammunition. Strachey examined one of the ultra-modern P-90's that looked like something from a science fiction movie. It was a far cry from the hand-me-down single-shot Sears .22 rifle that had been his first gun when he was ten. He had come a long way from Canton, North Carolina.

CHAPTER 28

Through the plane's window Strachey traced the silvery course of the Guadalquivir River and could see the glint of sun off the Atlantic some 50 miles in the distance as they descended from cruising altitude and banked left over Seville.

In the cockpit, the voice of the Seville air controller crackled in Nico Villagas' earphones. "Lear EC-JTZ, fly heading 270 and descend to 5,000 feet." Nico complied and 30 seconds later the controller informed him that San Pablo airport was at his 10 o'clock and ten miles distant. As soon as he spotted the airport off his left wing, Nico informed the controller and was given the frequency to contact the San Pablo tower.

He dropped to 4,000 feet on instructions from the tower and continued on a heading of 270 to vector into the field's airspace left downwind, heading for runway 9. At about a mile out, he banked the plane left and then left again to enter his glidepath and brought the LearJet 45 to a smooth landing.

The tower immediately instructed him to turn left at taxiway D and contact ground control on a different frequency to receive taxi instructions to the terminal building. A "Follow Me" car led them to a parking area near the main terminal.

As they came to a stop the four men in the passenger compartment re-packed the equipment Grant had brought from Langley into the two black nylon duffel bags and prepared to deplane as the engines wound down to a stop. Nico emerged from the cockpit and opened the hatch to let down the stairs. It was 11:30 AM on Thursday morning; tomorrow would be Christmas.

As soon as the group entered the VIP reception area, Gordi was on his cell-phone talking to the commander of the Seville Regional Brigade.

"Yes, of course I know that the investigation has been called off, but I'm still curious about what you discovered. You were supposed to have a full report ready for me this morning, after all. I'm just tying up loose ends here in Madrid."

He listened intently for several minutes, nodding occasionally, before ending the call and turning to the rest who were gathered in a tight group near the windows.

"It wasn't hard for the brigade to determine who owns that property," he said. "It's a pretty well-known local guy named Miguel Fernandez de Blanco. His family's been in Seville for centuries, and he owns half of Andalusia, and that's just a slight exaggeration. He has a clean reputation and seems like a quiet sort who minds his own business. He has a house in Seville, actually a small palace called the *Palacio del Infantado,* as well as the horse ranch, and he owns a small, but exclusive hotel in town, too."

"Not surprising," said Strachey after he had translated for Grant. "Whoever owns that ranch has to be wealthy, maybe wealthy enough to buy two nuclear bombs."

To Gordi, "Nothing negative cropped up in your guys' investigation? Nothing unusual?"

Gordi shook his head and pulled a face.

"He has a clean reputation."

"What do you think we should do, Alberto?" asked Strachey.

The *Comisario Principal* answered without hesitation.

"I don't think there's much of a choice. We have to get into that estate."

He surveyed the faces of Strachey and the others.

"No matter what happens," he finally said, "You heard what Sevillano said this morning. I have no authority to pry into Fernandez's business, or even to question him. Once I cross that line, I'm outside the law and I'm finished. I can't ask any of you to ..."

He didn't get farther than that.

Strachey said, "Alberto, we haven't come all this way to stop now, so don't start having second thoughts." Indicating Grant, he continued, "We're going to see this through to the end, and we have plenty of authority behind us."

Gordi placed a hand on Alberto's shoulder.

"*Amigito*, you couldn't get rid of me if you wanted to, and you know you're as helpless as a baby without me anyway."

Nico Villagas simply asked, "Will somebody give me a gun, *por favor*?"

Everybody stared at him for a moment and then burst out laughing as the tension broke.

"Nico," said Alberto, "we're not laughing at you, it's just that you always seem to know the right thing to say to let everybody relax."

Then more seriously, "I know you won't like this, but I want you to stay here at the airport. You need to refuel and be ready to take off again in a hurry. We may have to get somewhere fast, and you're our only ticket out of here."

Nico, who had undoubtedly fantasized throughout the flight about storming a terrorist hideout with guns blazing, was crestfallen and still smarted from the laughter his request had provoked. "You want me to stay behind and nursemaid the plane?"

Strachey stepped in.

"You won't be alone, Nico. We need a command post, and your plane is it. Mr. Grant here will stay with you to manage communications with Langley. If we run into serious trouble, we might have to call in some help. Plus, you speak English very well. You and

Mr. Grant will make a good team. It's an important job, Nico. You two are going to have our backs, and you'll be working with a Deputy Director of the CIA."

Mollified, Nico grumbled a bit more for form's sake, but raised no more objections.

The group split up, with Strachey, Alberto, and Gordi heading for the car rental counter. Grant and Nico returned to the plane to set up the communications gear provided by Langley that included an encrypted sat-phone to match the one Strachey carried, a remote satellite receiving station to which KH-11 imagery could be downloaded, and a laptop computer equipped with sophisticated encryption software that would allow them to send and receive data from Langley in real time using the LearJet-45's satellite link. Strachey and Grant also carried identical, encrypted cell-phones to provide communications redundancy.

*****

Ten kilometers away from the airport, the streamlined Talgo 350 AVE bullet train from Madrid came to a hissing stop in Seville's ultra-modern Santa Justa Station at the same time Nico's jet was landing. Ricardo Sevillano helped his wife and two children onto the platform. They had barely made it to Madrid's Atocha Station for the 300 kmh train's departure at 9:00 AM.

Sevillano herded his family along the

platform and up the escalator toward the exits through the throng of holiday travelers. He spotted the waiting white Mercedes sedan immediately. The driver, Fernandez's young son, Miguel, got out and helped pack the luggage in the trunk while Sevillano's wife loaded the children into the back seat. Sevillano sat in front, next to Miguel.

"I didn't think we were going to make the train. What a nightmare! What does your father plan to do now?

"Nothing's changed. The plan goes forward."

"But the Iranian ..."

"That's been taken care of. The second package is already on its way, and the first, as you know, has been in place for several days already. We're still on schedule." He reached across and patted Sevillano's shoulder. "My father says you did a marvelous job in Madrid. We could have lost everything."

Sevillano grunted. He agreed. He HAD done a marvelous job in Madrid, and in two days' time, even less now, the world would be changed forever.

The white Mercedes cleared the city and sped westward.

*****

At the airport Strachey rented a Citroën C4 compact sedan, a modest car that would not attract attention and easily accommodated the three men plus the equipment. It would take them less than an hour to reach Aznalcazar, plus another fifteen minutes or so to locate the ranch. Langley had supplied a portable GPS system, and Strachey already had the coordinates loaded.

CHAPTER 29

They navigated the Holiday traffic westward along the *Autopista del Quinto Centenario*, the arid, sunbaked hills of Andalusia with their gray-green scrub vegetation blurring past before reaching the turn-off south and entering a narrow macadamed road that led them through seemingly endless olive and almond groves. It took another ten minutes to reach the picturesque town of Aznalcazar, bordered on the west by the meandering clear waters of the Guadiamar River. The Fernandez hacienda lay a further 8 kilometers south according to the GPS.

They had used the travel time to devise a strategy and now selected a route that would take them along the west bank of the river to a point opposite the entrance to the ranch that sat on the east bank. The tranquil river banks were thick with trees, and they would be completely shielded from observation from the secluded hacienda.

Ten minutes after leaving Aznalcazar Strachey pulled to the side of the road just as he completed a cell phone conversation with Grant, finally steering the Citroën more deeply into a thick stand of trees, and killing the engine. "Grant confirms that we have dedicated surveillance satellite coverage," he said, "and he's downloading the live feed right now. There's very little activity in the area, but a white sedan arrived about a half-hour ago. Two men, a woman, and two children entered the main house, and it's been quiet ever since."

"Is there any sign of the blue Mercedes the Iranian was driving?" asked Alberto.

"Nothing, but there are a number of outbuildings and it could be under cover."

Their plan was necessarily makeshift with many variables that would require improvisation when the time came. With no knowledge of the manpower (or firepower) that could be waiting for them in Fernandez's compound Strachey had ruled out a frontal assault. A close up reconnaissance of the enemy was called for, and there was only one way it could be done effectively, but it could well turn out to be a suicide mission.

Strachey opened the door of the Citroën and stepped out into the pleasant Andalusian air. The other two followed. The secluded clearing apparently was used for camping, perhaps by the gypsy caravans that were common in this part of the country. Strachey walked back out to the road and could see no traffic in either direction.

When he returned he found Alberto and Gordi involved in a heated exchange, and could readily guess what it was about. Gordi had been grumbling ever since the plan was formulated. They quieted down at Strachey's approach, although Gordi's face bore a chagrined expression.

"I still don't like it," he said. "It should be me who goes. Alberto is the one who knows everything. If they captured me, they could learn very little."

This wasn't true, and Gordi had to know his argument was weak. He had been briefed on everything Alberto had learned about the alleged Fernandez plan, and he had been a part of the operation since they had met in Alberto's office that morning.

"*Joder*, Gordi," said Alberto. "You're a better shot than me, and you know it. Besides, I have nothing professionally to lose if this turns out to be a wild goose chase. It's logical that I go in. It's settled."

And it was true: Gordi had been a member of the GEO paramilitary squad during his early, thinner years with the CNP and had participated in his share of armed raids on ETA hideouts. When his burgeoning girth and age began to affect his performance, he had transferred to the intelligence unit. None of them really believed that their actions today would be resolved peacefully, and Gordi's experience could best be applied by remaining with Strachey.

Strachey and Alberto still wore the suits and ties they had started the day with at the Presidential Palace. The Spaniard now removed his suit jacket, laid it carefully on the hood of the car and rolled up his shirt sleeve. Gordi stood by glumly observing as Strachey retrieved one of the black duffel bags from the trunk and began rummaging through it. He found what he wanted and extracted a small black plastic case from the bag. Placing the case on the hood of the car next to Alberto's jacket he opened it to reveal adark foam lining with slots cut to fit the pieces of gear stowed inside. Strachey applied a 2x2-inch flesh colored patch to Alberto's upper right arm. He then handed him a tiny ear bud made of clear, malleable plastic that would fit completely inside his ear and would be impossible to detect without a very thorough physical examination.

After checking to make certain the ear bud was completely invisible, the CIA man said, "As I explained, the patch looks exactly like a regular bandage, and I've placed it where a bandage might be used to cover a recent vaccination. It conceals some micro-circuitry and a power source even I didn't know existed. The ear bud works two ways, you hear what we say, and we hear everything that you hear and say. The patch conceals the transceiver and has a range of about a mile. It's the very best we have, and I think it has a good chance of not being noticed in a body search if it comes to that."

The Spaniard nodded his understanding and rolled down his sleeve. "OK, *vamos!*"

He gave Strachey a firm Spanish *abrazo*, embrace, and then turned to Gordi. "I'm not worried, *amigo*, because I know you've got my back."

Gordi choked out, "*Vaya con Dios, amigo*," as he hugged his friend.

Alberto put his jacket back on and climbed into the car behind the wheel. Gordi and the American stood mutely as he disappeared down the road still heading south. He would re-cross the river and turn north at an intersection onto a road that would take him to the entrance of Fernandez's compound on the other side of the river.

Strachey said, "Let's suit up," and he and Gordi headed back to where the two duffel bags waited on the ground. As they walked the American called Grant. "Have you got him in sight?"

*****

At San Pablo airport Grant sat with Nico in the LearJet's passenger compartment. Nico had bought two large paper cups of strong black Spanish coffee, and the two were glued to the real time KH-11 satellite image on the laptop's screen. "Yes, he's nearing the bridge at *Cordel de Camino* now."

They followed the Citroën's progress as it

turned northward at the bridge over the Guadiamar and finally turned into the compound's gated entrance.

CHAPTER 30

It was nearly 2:00 PM when Alberto pulled the Citroën up to the wrought iron gates beside the metal call box mounted on a post on the driver's side. Nothing could be seen of the house or outbuildings through a dense grove of olive trees. Before he could push the call button a voice came from the speaker. "This is private property. What do you want?"

Alberto held his police identification up to the camera lens. *"Comisario Principal* Alberto Macías on police business to see Sr. Miguel Fernandez."

"Sr. Fernandez is not receiving visitors."

"I'm not a visitor. As I said, I'm here on official police business. Open the gate."

After a pause, the disembodied voice said, "Please wait a moment." Five minutes passed as Alberto considered the few other options they had to penetrate the compound. They had no idea how many people might be inside or how they might be armed, and a frontal assault was the least appetizing possibility. Surreptitious entry was an option. The grounds and fields surrounding the compound were extensive, possibly thousands of acres of farm and grazing lands, and they couldn't have the entire area wired against intruders. The KH-11 coverage already had given them the lay of the land but could not see into the buildings. The best opportunity to gather the intelligence they needed was what he was doing right now – on the ground reconnaissance and personal confrontation with Fernandez. Walking into the lion's den was not the most appetizing choice, but no other ploy offered them a better chance to find out what they desperately needed to know.

He looked up at a sound. The gates were swinging open. The voice from the speaker said, "Follow the drive to the house."

Alberto drew a deep breath and put the car into gear. The graveled drive was long and wound through the olive grove for at least a quarter mile before yielding sight of the house. As he entered the compound, Alberto scanned the outbuildings, a stable, a barn, and various utility sheds. He noted especially a concrete building that looked like a bunker with a large generator at its side. The wide central doors of the barn were open and inside he could discern a parked dark colored Mercedes with Madrid plates. "It looks like the Iranians' car is here," he said for Strachey's ears, knowing that the CIA man was monitoring the receiving equipment for the transmitter he was wearing. "It's under cover in the barn." He began to hope that Shirazi was still there.

The hacienda itself was a large, L-shaped white stucco structure of one story with a red tile roof and a circular drive in the V of the two wings. He pulled to a stop behind a white Mercedes, took another deep breath to compose himself, and stepped out of the Citroën.

Now it began.

The main entrance was at the intersection of the two wings and consisted of huge paneled oak double doors. One of the doors was opened as he approached by a burly, unsmiling gentleman with unfriendly eyes wearing a white servant's jacket that was stretched tightly over an athletic frame. The olive skinned man towered over Alberto, and his head was shaved and oiled to shiny perfection. He looked more like a bodyguard or professional wrestler than a house servant.

The man stood aside and mutely gestured for Alberto to enter. The tiled foyer was pleasantly cool and Alberto could see that the house's two wings were separated by a wide central hallway that went completely through to the rear where a sliding glass door led out to a patio. He could make out a swimming pool beyond shimmering in the bright sun of early afternoon. Somewhere a fountain was tinkling.

He heard the door close behind him and

turned from his inspection of the interior to be confronted by the .45 caliber muzzle of a gun held by the servant who had admitted him. He recognized the weapon as a Heckler & Koch Mark 23. The pistol, originally developed for the U.S. Special Operations Command, looked small in the man's meaty hand.

Maintaining his *sang-froid*, Alberto demanded, "What's the meaning of this? I'm a police officer. Put that weapon away." Such an eventuality was not entirely unexpected.

*****

On the other side of the river where they were listening intently, Gordi leapt to his feet. "He's in trouble already! This was a lousy idea."

Strachey held out a calming hand. "Take it easy, Gordi. We never thought it would be easy. If they were going to shoot him, they would have done it by now. They're undoubtedly curious. Remember, Alberto is on an intelligence gathering mission. We discussed this possibility."

Strachey now wore a Navy special ops TRU (Tactical Response Uniform) of a blue so dark it appeared black to the naked eye, complete with body armor and a tactical equipment vest. Shoved into the cross draw holster of his tactical vest under his left arm was an FN Five-Seven pistol to match the P-90 submachine gun slung over his back. There was a uniform for Gordi, too, but his girth had proven too much for it, although the vest adjustments did permit him to wear it with the Velcro straps at their extreme limits. Fortunately, his feet were not of an inconvenient size, and the extra boots in the kit fit him perfectly. He had discarded his service pistol in favor of the same weapons as Strachey.

CHAPTER 31

A second man who could have been the twin of the first except that he sported a full head of bushy black hair entered the foyer from the main hallway behind Alberto. "Hands behind your head," he ordered.

While the first thug kept his weapon aimed at Alberto's midsection, the second patted him down, removing the Spaniard's service pistol and leather holster from his belt and dropping them in his own pocket. The man was well experienced in the art of the body search and checked all of Alberto's pockets, turning them inside out and collecting what he retrieved in a neat pile beside a vase of flowers on an antique table that stood along one wall with a mirror behind it. Looking at the scene reflected in the mirror Alberto saw a wiry 5'7" Spaniard with his hands grasped behind his neck sandwiched between two six foot plus gorillas.

Playing the role of the outraged official to perfection, Alberto said, "This is unacceptable. You've seen my credentials and you know I'm a policeman. You're breaking the law, and I'll see that you pay for it."

The man with the gun only smirked and wagged the barrel toward the rear of the house, and the second roughly jerked him around and shoved him forward with a flat palm between his shoulder blades.

"I demand to see Sr. Miguel Rodriguez immediately," said Alberto in his best official voice as he stumbled forward, still prodded by the big man's hand.

"Sr. Rodriguez is having lunch and will decide whether or not he wants to see you when he is finished."

The man spoke with a heavy accent that seemed familiar.

He wondered what they planned to do if Rodriguez decided he didn't want to see him.

They led him to a door on the right three-quarters of the way down the length of the corridor and shoved him inside what he surmised was a servants' service preparation area. He could see a large, white tiled kitchen through an opening in the far wall where the prepared dishes would be handed through. The clatter and banging one would normally expect from a busy kitchen was absent, however, and the place seemed deserted. There was a table along one black and white tiled wall where he was instructed to sit. The bald man who had opened the front door sat opposite, keeping the H&K pointed at him, while the second left the room, closing the door behind him.

Alberto weighed about 150 pounds soaking wet and he judged that his captor had him by at least a hundred pounds plus a very large gun. There was no question of taking the guy on physically, so he decided to see how smart his captor was while at the same time transmitting more information to Strachey and Gordi.

The huge man's olive skin was unusually dark, even for a Spaniard from Andalusia, and there was something about his nose that didn't look quite right.

Recalling the man's accented Spanish, Alberto asked, "How long have you been in Spain?"

The thug just stared at him.

Alberto persisted, "You don't look Spanish and you don't sound Spanish, so how long have you been here?"

No response.

With a glance at the corridor door, Alberto said, "Look, *amigo*, lunch could last a long time. We might as well talk to one another or you might get so bored you'll fall asleep, and how would Sr. Fernandez like that?"

"There is no possibility that I will fall asleep."

As he said this, the man raised the pistol and aimed it directly between Alberto's eyes.

"See?" said Alberto, "We can have a conversation. I wonder if you know how much trouble you're in right now."

"Looks to me like YOU'RE the one in trouble."

"Now we're really talking! So, tell me how long you've been in Spain."

"What makes you think I haven't always been here?" The thug lowered the pistol so the butt rested on the table, level with Alberto's chest.

"Not with that accent."

Now the thug was insulted.

"I speak perfect Spanish."

"I'm sure anyone might believe that until you opened your mouth."

"Fuck you."

"Fuck you, too," replied Alberto amicably. "Now, why don't you just tell me where you're from? After all, it won't make much difference, will it?"

The man revealed large, white teeth in a nasty grin.

"You know something? You can count on that. One more day, and nothing anyone says or does will make any difference."

Finally, a solid clue. So they had another day before anything would happen. Alberto hoped Strachey had picked up on what had been said.

"What's that supposed to mean?"

It occurred belatedly to the thug that he may have said too much.

"Wouldn't you like to know?" he said and

flushed with embarrassment at his childish rejoinder.

"Is that the best you can do?"

Alberto leaned back in the wooden chair.

"'Wouldn't you like to know?'" he mimicked the man's words and his accent in a childlike voice.

The thug's eyes narrowed and he started to rise from his chair.

"Fuck you," he snarled.

"Again, fuck you, too, but where you are from you usually fuck sheep, don't you?"

At last he had pegged the man's accent. He'd heard it before, and not too many days ago.

The thug half rose and Alberto wondered if he had gone too far in provoking him, but with an obvious effort the behemoth eased himself back into his chair.

Still seething, he said, "You know nothing of where I am from. You are a pathetic, skinny little Spanish bastard who is unlikely to see tomorrow's sunrise."

"I seriously doubt that that decision belongs to you."

Alberto kept his voice even, without a trace of animosity.

"And so why don't we talk about something else? Why don't you tell me about the last time you saw Tehran?"

The man attempted to conceal his surprise, but Alberto knew he had hit the mark. Shirazi had spoken Spanish well, but with certain inflections that the Spaniard belatedly had recognized in the thug's speech. This was yet another nail in a coffin that Alberto sincerely hoped would not become his own. The thug displayed all the characteristics of a soldier, and Alberto suspected he could be a member of the Revolutionary Guard Corps, the elite troops of Iran. Put this together with what Shirazi had told them and the appearance of the VEVAK operative and there was more than enough evidence to convince even the Spanish government to take immediate action. If only he had been permitted to carry through with his initial plans they would have had a chance. Now he had to ensure that Strachey was warned.

"You look and act like a soldier," he said. "Are you and your twin from the Revolutionary Guard Corps, the *Pasdaran*?"

The thug smiled thinly, his small eyes gleaming at the small Spaniard who sat opposite him. He said nothing.

"So," pursued Alberto, "if you're from the Revolutionary Guard does that mean you're authorized to fuck goats instead of sheep, or do you just sodomize one another in the barracks?"

"Silence!" roared the big man, looking like he was going to pull the trigger this time. "You infidel son of a pig," the Iranian grated, "you are an inferior little man of an inferior, barbarian race, and you'll learn soon enough what being fucked really means! If you say another word, I'll break your arm."

He meant it, and Alberto knew it, but he had elicited important information. He only hoped that Strachey had heard everything.

Strachey's urgent plea reached him through the ear bud. "We got it, Alberto. Now, for Chris' sake, just keep your mouth shut for a while."

They sat in silence for another half-hour, the Iranian fuming all the while, until the corridor door opened. The second guard poked his head in and said, "Sr. Fernandez will see him now."

CHAPTER 32

Thanks to flawlessly functioning equipment, something that surprised Strachey, he could follow everything happening inside the house and was transmitting the audio feed to Grant at San Pablo Airport who was relaying it simultaneously to Langley, providing everyone involved with real-time coverage of what was happening inside Fernandez's compound.

Strachey's admiration for Alberto Macías had grown to gargantuan proportions. Everyone had known that this was a suicide mission for Alberto, and the plucky Spanish cop had walked calmly into the belly of the beast. His phlegmatic acceptance of his duty was inspiring, and he was fulfilling his intelligence collection mission. The meeting with Miguel Fernandez was a critical part of that mission, but success was far from assured. From this point on everything was improvisation and depended on Alberto's proven elicitation skills.

Strachey resolved that Alberto Macías would not die, or at the very least would not die alone, and that meant that at some point in the very near future he and Gordi would be entering that compound.

*****

The two Iranian goons led Alberto back out into the house's central corridor and toward the main entrance foyer. Earlier, he had noted that there were two doorways, one to the right of the entrance to the corridor, and one on the left. When they reached the foyer, goon number two (the one with hair) knocked softly on the door on the left and a faint voice could be heard inviting them inside.

They passed into yet another vestibule, a room about twelve feet by twelve, tastefully decorated with wall hangings, a large mirror and antiques. Broad French doors with old glass panels opened into a huge living room that stretched all the way to the back of the house where a picture window provided a view of grazing horses in a distant pasture and a kidney-shaped swimming pool that occupied half of a large, flagstoned veranda. The room itself was richly carpeted, and its walls were adorned with more wall hangings that Alberto recognized as Belgian *gobelins*, likely several centuries old. On the wall to his left was a huge stone fireplace and above it a display of ancient bladed weapons.

A large, glass-topped coffee table sat in front of a long, handsomely upholstered couch with its back to the picture window, and a trim man of about sixty with smooth, well-tanned patrician features, dressed in tan gabardine trousers, a white dress shirt and green silk cravat was seated on the couch with his legs crossed. Alberto assumed that this must be his "host," Miguel Fernandez.

Standing beside Fernandez was a younger man in white chinos and a light cotton sweater whose features showed unmistakably that he was the older man's son. But it was the third person in the room, seated next to Fernandez, which caused Alberto to stop cold in his tracks. One of the goons shoved him forward until he stood on one side of the coffee table facing the couch.

"What do you think you're doing here, Macías," growled the Director of the National Police.

Alberto found his voice. "Director Sevillano, I might ask you the same."

"You should have stayed away, Macías, and done as you were told. Now it's too late for you."

"Would you care to explain that remark, Director?"

"It should be self-evident." Sevillano eyed Alberto suspiciously. "Did you come alone, or do you have anybody with you -- maybe your CIA friends?"

Alberto said, "You made certain that I had

no friends, Director, remember?"

"I don't believe you." Pointing at the baldheaded guard Sevillano said, "Get the men and do a thorough sweep. Make sure you don't miss anything."

In his ear Strachey's disembodied voice whispered to Alberto, "We heard that, Alberto. Don't worry. They won't find us until we want them to. This will give us a chance to find out how many of them there are."

"Look all you want," said Alberto over his shoulder to the retreating back of the bald-headed Iranian. "There's no one there."

For the first time Miguel Fernandez spoke.

"Why are you here, *Comisario* Macías? What did you think you would accomplish?"

"I came to stop a mad man from committing mass murder."

Fernandez didn't look like a mad man. In fact, he was utterly composed as he studied the man his guards had brought before him. He hadn't changed his relaxed position as Sevillano and Alberto talked, but now he uncrossed his legs and leaned forward with his elbows on his knees, directing his entire attention on the *Comisario Principal.*

"Are you a student of history, *Comisario?*"

"Not particularly."

"That's a shame. Everyone should know at least their own history. Then tell me what you think about ethnic cleansing. Do you think it is ever justified?"

"No, of course not."

"Oh," said Fernandez with a smile, "but your views on the subject are those of an enlightened 21st Century European. You might not have felt the same a few hundred years ago."

"We're not having this conversation a few hundred years ago."

"You are correct, of course, but some wounds remain forever open. Your ancestors, *Comisario*, committed heinous crimes and atrocities against innocents, their only reason being a difference of religion mixed with a certain amount of greed. Surely you've heard of Tomás de Torquemada?"

"Of course."

If it gained them time Alberto would play this game as long as Fernandez liked.

"Yes, a name to conjure up nightmares, isn't it? He was Queen Isabella's confessor and the first Grand Inquisitor. Did you know that his grandmother was Jewish, actually a *converso*, a Jew who had converted to Christianity? Do you think that somehow might have increased his zeal to burn people at the stake or strip their skin from them in his torture chambers?"

"I wouldn't know."

"I think it must have," mused Fernandez almost as if he were talking to himself. "He seemed to enjoy the screams and the smell of roasting flesh so much, he and his successors."

Alberto allowed his frustration to show.

"I didn't come here to discuss ancient

history."

Fernandez smiled benignly.

"You may not have realized it, but that's exactly why you're here. This is ALL about 'ancient history,' as you call it."

Alberto needed information, not a history lesson.

"Sr. Fernandez, do you intend to detonate a nuclear device somewhere in Spain?"

Fernandez went silent for a long second, his eyebrows knitted.

"My, but you have come with the most interesting questions, *Comisario*, questions about 'mass murder,' and now nuclear devices."

Alberto needed an answer.

"Director Sevillano certainly knows what I'm talking about, and I don't doubt he's filled you in on our meeting this morning in Madrid."

Sevillano interjected, "We should kill him now, Sultan."

Alberto looked from the police Director to Fernandez.

"Sultan?"

Fernandez flashed a censorious look at Sevillano and made a shushing sound as he would to a child who had spoken out of turn. Then, his attention back on Alberto, he asked, "Where are you from, Macías? Where did you grow up?"

"You answer my question first."

Ignoring him, Fernandez stood and walked to the fireplace where he removed one of the weapons from the wall. "Do you know what this is, Macías?"

"It appears to be a sword."

Fernandez frowned slightly and flicked the blade before him in the air so it made a swishing noise.

"Any schoolchild would give that answer," he said. "This is a genuine Spanish rapier with a *Taza* cup hilt. Its blade was forged in Toledo in the first half of the 17th century. An identical weapon was once used by another Spaniard who invaded my family's home in Seville."

He carefully replaced the weapon on the wall and turned again to Alberto.

"Your life may depend on your answer to this question, *Comisario.* Where are you from originally?"

"Will you answer my question if I answer yours?"

Alberto felt the Iranian guard's big hands grip his arms more tightly from behind.

Fernandez sighed again and returned to his seat on the couch.

"Yes, *Comisario,* I suppose I will, but believe me, your answer will be much more important to your continued well-being than mine."

"I'm from Sepúlveda, not far from Segóvia. Why is that of any importance?"

"Bear with me. Has your family been there long?"

"As long as anyone can remember."

Fernandez nodded.

"The irony is really quite astonishing – perhaps even an omen."

Alberto had had enough of the older man's doubletalk.

"Now, you answer my question. Do you intend to detonate a nuclear device somewhere in Spain?"

Fernandez considered this for a moment.

"Sattar," he said, addressing the guard who still held tightly to the Spaniard's arms, "take our guest to the bunker and lock him in. Don't mistreat him, and make sure he has something to eat and drink. Post a guard outside."

The Iranian started to turn Alberto back toward the door, but he resisted.

"You agreed to answer my question if I answered yours," he said over his shoulder as the guard hustled him toward to door.

"I did, and the answer is yes."

CHAPTER 33

Strachey was on the phone with Grant. "Can you see anything yet?"

"Yes, I've counted five men, all of them armed, coming out of the house. They've begun a sweep of the property. Another one has just come out with Alberto. He's taking him toward the concrete bunker."

"Is there any indication that they might come across the river?"

"An SUV just came out of the barn, and someone is getting into the white Mercedes." A moment passed before Grant's voice sounded again in Strachey's ear. "The SUV is heading south toward the bridge, and the Mercedes is going in the opposite direction."

Strachey could see the cars through the trees. He turned to Gordi.

"They'll be patrolling this side of the river in a couple of minutes. We've got to get under cover.

Just in case, screw the silencer onto your P-90."

He extracted the black cylinder of the Gemtech silencer from his tactical vest as they retreated into the trees that lined the river bank. They scrambled down and lay on their bellies under some thick bushes, having concealed the two duffle bags behind a log.

"They've crossed over and are driving slowly now. They should be at your position within a few minutes," said Grant, relaying information from the KH-11 image on his computer screen.

Strachey and Gordi heard the SUV before they saw it as it rolled slowly along the road. The man in the passenger seat stared intently into the foliage, but they didn't stop.

"They're turning around," reported Grant a minute later.

Strachey suspected that having completed their initial search the two men in the car would now inspect the river bank on foot. It's what he would have done.

They were stationed directly across the river from the compound. Either the guards would choose that point to begin their sweep on foot, in which case they might split up and go in opposite directions, or they would stop farther along and walk together.

"They're headed back toward your position," reported Grant.

"Get ready," whispered Strachey to Gordi.

He didn't want to start shooting now in broad daylight. It was only mid-afternoon.

Tactically, it would have been better to wait until later for Alberto to go to the house, but the pressing need to discover where the bomb was located had outweighed that.

The SUV crunched to a stop on the road directly in front of their position. Their vision was limited by the foliage, but Strachey saw the two men exit their vehicle and begin walking toward the river. Both carried Russian PP2000 submachine guns, the latest and deadliest product of the KPB Instrument Design Bureau and more than a match for the lightweight Belgian P-90's that Strachey and Gordi carried. No more than ten yards now separated them.

The two entered the camp site clearing and immediately spotted the fresh tire tracks left by the Citroën. They each took a knee and carefully scanned the tree line. Strachey held his breath. They had scuffed up the ground in the clearing enough to indicate that more than one person had been there, and Strachey silently cursed himself for having failed to erase those telltale marks. One of the men reached for a walkie-talkie that hung from his belt, undoubtedly to report what they had discovered and call in reinforcements, and that was the last thing Strachey could afford this early in the game.

He set the P-90's fire selection control to the "A" position for fully automatic fire, nudged Gordi and the two of them stood and dropped the two intruders in a hail of 5.7X28mm bullets before they could return fire. Strachey, who had fired the weapon only once during training, was still amazed at the relatively low recoil, even on full automatic. He had emptied at least half of the 50-round magazine and never lost his sight picture.

He had not intended to set an ambush, but that's the way it had turned out, and now they faced a serious problem. The men they had just shot would be expected to report in with the results of their reconnaissance and when they didn't the alarm would be raised. If they were to achieve an advantage by surprise, they would have to act now.

Strachey contacted Grant to report while Gordi examined the bodies.

"We have to go in now. Can you give me some positions?"

"Just a moment. They've scattered across the property, and it's hard to keep track of all of them. If we counted correctly there should be at least five guards left to deal with. There may be more, but we counted seven for sure, including the one who had Alberto. He's now posted himself outside the bunker."

Their first objective would be to rescue Alberto.

"Where is the bunker in relation to the house?"

"Beside the barn on the left, across from the house, where the SUV was parked – the same place Alberto spotted the blue Mercedes. A guard is standing in front of it."

"Gordi, we're going to have to split up. Do

you think you can get into the compound without being seen?"

"It won't be easy in broad daylight."

"What if I create a diversion to draw the guards' attention?"

Strachey outlined his plan and gave Gordi enough time to wade across the river and find concealment on the other bank while he filled in Grant.

"The drive to the house is quite long," said Grant, almost a quarter mile, and I can see one guard who has taken up position about twenty yards inside the gate. You'll have to be fast."

Strachey could tell from the tone of Grant's voice that he was worried and not entirely convinced the plan would work.

"Remember the primary objective, Bob."

"Harvey, this is our only chance, and we don't have any more time."

"I know, and we won't get another one if you get yourself killed."

"I don't believe in suicide missions. Keep your eyes on the KH-11 stuff and keep me posted on what you see. I'm tying the cell phones into our tactical commo. Have Nico translate into Spanish if you see something Gordi and Alberto need to hear."

"Will do. Good luck, Bob. I'm saying a prayer."

"I'll need all the help I can get, and some Divine intervention would be welcome."

He carried the two duffle bags and the

Russian submachine guns he had retrieved from the two bodies out to the road where the SUV was parked. It was a Range Rover 10MY, the biggest one sold in Spain, and the badge on its side boasted a powerful diesel V8 twin-turbo engine that should be more than sufficient for what he had in mind. He tossed the bags into the back and climbed behind the wheel.

"Are you ready, Gordi?"

"Ready," came the Spaniard's voice crackling with tension through his ear bud.

"Have you been listening, Alberto?"

"Not much else to do in here," replied Alberto. "Bring a gun for me."

CHAPTER 34

The Spanish network of modern highways is a superb example of rational planning and execution for the rapid modernization of a country. Thanks to this marvel of post-Franco Spain, Colonel Zarin and his unwilling passenger traversed nearly the entire country to arrive at their destination a mere nine hours after their hasty departure from Aznalcazar.

León, located in the far northwest corner of the country has been in existence for over 2,000 years, originally established as a military camp for the Roman Sixth Legion in the first century A.D. It has seen many changes and many battles across the centuries and today is a bustling, prosperous provincial center that boasts magnificent architectural and historic monuments, a fine cathedral, energetic industry, and wine from vines planted originally by the Roman Legionnaires. It is home to nearly 140,000 people.

At four o'clock in the afternoon on Christmas Eve Zarin drove the truck into town via the *Avenida de Fernandez Ladreda*, then circled the bullring until they entered the *Paseo de Papalagunida* that took them north, parallel with the Bernesga River that bisects the city, finally turning into the parking area at the Parador Nacional de San Marcos, formerly the Convent of San Marcos. The original building was torn down in the 16th Century, and the current building was put in its place, thanks to a generous donation from King Fernando the Catholic. In its time, the massive stone pile has seen many uses, from convent to prison to stables, and is now one of a national string of five-star hotels created from historical sites during the Franco years. The large parking area is outside, ideal to guarantee maximum effect from a nuclear explosion. Though not precisely at the city's center that lays to the east, the device's initial kill radius of three miles would be more than sufficient to lay it to waste, and the main government building of the province, the *Delegación de la Junta en León*, is just across the street.

Inside the canvas covered cargo area, carefully secured and linked to a series of 12-volt batteries that comprised its external power supply the Russian landmine rested like a gray larva.

Shirazi's anxiety rose to a high pitch as they made their way into the city through streets bedecked in Holiday finery. He could not expel from his thoughts images of the devastation the device would inflict. Everything within a third of a mile of ground zero would be vaporized instantly in a boiling hot flash that would reach some 540,000 degrees Fahrenheit. Thousands would die instantly, and still more thousands within a matter of seconds. The explosion would produce huge amounts of radioactive fallout particles that the winds would disperse over a large area. Those not immediately killed would see the intense blinding flash from the thermal pulse just before the blast overpressure hit them. All transportation - cars, trains, planes - would be incapacitated by the electromagnetic pulse emanating from the detonation site. Tens of thousands of people would die painfully from the delayed reaction of radiation sickness. The subsequent chaos would be unimaginable.

Shirazi feared for his soul. Could God really consider such carnage a holy duty?

Zarin selected a corner of the nearly empty lot and backed into a space so the rear was concealed. There were few people about due to the Holidays, and he did not fear discovery. He walked to the passenger side and ordered Shirazi out then shoved him to the rear where they opened the canvas flap.

"Get in and do what you were intended by God to do, and pray He will forgive your attempted treachery."

Zarin drew a pistol from his belt.

Still trembling, Shirazi put his foot on the lower rung of the small metal stepladder appended to the truck's bumper and climbed up. The huge landmine sat in the semi-darkness waiting for him like some malevolent subterranean creature waiting to spring from its lair. A tool kit sat near the device's access hatch.

With a heavy wrench he removed the bolts that held the access hatch cover flush with the casing and then leaned the cover against the side of the truck. Inside the device, behind the trigger mechanism and control panel was a tangle of wires and the central plutonium reservoir surrounded by a ring of shaped explosives. Shirazi connected the trigger mechanism to the landmine's internal systems and ran a diagnostic test.

"Hurry up," hissed Zarin. "We have a schedule to keep. If you are thinking of not setting the trigger properly or anything of that sort, remember that your family will pay dearly for such a failure."

Shirazi was bereft of choices. He would do as ordered and pray for forgiveness. He did not expect to live for much longer, but there was hope for his wife and daughters.

Turning back to address Zarin, he said, "This can't be rushed. The diagnostic will take at least five minutes before I can begin to set the trigger."

Although the landmine was capable of remote detonation the Russian seller had been unable to supply the equipment required, forcing them to rely on the mechanical timer. It was a decades-old mechanism, he knew, that might well self-detonate at the slightest provocation. He toyed momentarily with the idea of detonating the weapon now, killing himself and the odious blond VEVAK Colonel along with the rest, but his courage failed him. And so he came to the final unalterable step. Following Zarin' terse instructions, he entered the access code and set the device to detonate at midnight.

It was five o'clock and the sun was beginning to set when the two Iranians walked out of the parking lot and around to the front of the hotel where they found a taxi to take them to the airport.

CHAPTER 35

Strachey checked his watch as he approached the turn-off for the entrance to the Fernandez compound. It was 3:30 PM, not the most propitious hour for a frontal assault.

Grant reported that the satellite coverage still showed the guard posted inside the gate plus another two who were now patrolling the front perimeter inside the wall.

He translated this for Gordi.

"Those two will be yours to handle. Can you do it?"

"*Si*, don't worry. You're within sight of the entrance now."

The rotund Spanish cop was concealed in the foliage directly opposite the entrance.

Drawing up to the turn, Strachey pulled into the drive and saw the ornate cast iron gates ahead, judging them to be some five yards from the road. He stopped the SUV and backed it to the opposite side of the road to gain more distance.

"Ready?"

"I'm already behind you," said Gordi, who had emerged onto the road and now crouched directly behind the huge SUV.

"Here we go!"

Strachey put the SUV into low gear and mashed the gas pedal to the floor sending the big vehicle careering up the drive toward the gates. He had his window rolled down and the P-90 in his left hand ready to fire. The powerful SUV crashed through the gates, splitting them open with a terrific clang, but barely slowed. A quick check of the rear view mirror showed Gordi chugging gamely up to the entrance with his P-90 at the ready.

A guard leapt into the drive ahead of him, leveling his weapon at the oncoming SUV, and Strachey's P-90 sprayed fully automatic death at him. There was no way the CIA man could be accurate under such conditions, firing with one hand, and he struggled to keep the recoil from riding the barrel up, but he was counting on his 900 rounds per minute rate of fire to do the job, and he was not disappointed. At least a few rounds must have struck the mark because the man went down. Whether he was mortally wounded at that point made no difference as Strachey ran the SUV directly over him and felt two distinct bumps as a front and a rear tire finished the job.

"The cavalry's on the way, Alberto. Get ready."

Strachey's first objective was to release Alberto and he still had considerable ground to cover before he would reach the complex of buildings that included the bunker. He shifted into a higher gear and sped forward. Machine guns rattled behind him as Gordi engaged the other guards. The Spaniard had removed the silencer from his weapon, and the sound of gunfire would attract the remaining guards to the front of the property. Strachey hoped they wouldn't come running down the drive but take a more direct route through the olive groves.

The SUV careened into the courtyard that divided the main house from the outbuildings and stood precariously on two wheels as Strachey whipped the wheel left toward the bunker. He caught a quick glimpse of the rented Citroën still parked in front of the house as he raced past. Alberto's guard was momentarily confused by the gunfire in the distance and the sudden appearance of the SUV that he assumed still carried his own men. Assumptions can kill, and before the man could react Strachey had brought the SUV to a screeching halt right in front of the bunker and dropped him. At such close range none of Strachey's shots missed and ten of the P-90's small caliber bullets cartwheeled in organ destroying circles through his chest. Strachey could hear a furious firefight from behind him at the gate.

Scanning his field of view as he leapt from the SUV, Strachey could see no one else in the immediate vicinity. On the bunker's door was a large padlock the key to which Strachey found in the dead man's pocket. As he struggled to get the key into the lock with one hand he caught a movement to his right as another guard appeared from around the corner of the house, and rounds slammed into the side of the SUV and pinged off the bunker's concrete to the right of the door.

Strachey had shifted the P-90 to his right hand, extended his arm in the direction of the guard and squeezed the trigger. Still on full automatic the compact weapon spit out another ten rounds and quit, its 50-round magazine exhausted from the initial assault. Strachey worried that Teacher had sent enough ammunition. The small caliber of the P90 rounds required multiple shots for a kill.

"Hold on, Alberto. I have something else to take care of right now."

He needed both hands to replace the spent magazine with a new one and slipped the key into his pocket as he took cover. Crouching behind the SUV he grabbed another flat magazine from his tactical vest. As he did so several rounds from his attacker's weapon ripped completely through the sturdy body of the SUV and planted themselves in the side of the bunker behind him. The guard's 9mm PP2000 was firing special overpressure ammunition that could penetrate armor. He scrambled quickly to the front of the

SUV to get behind the engine block as he slammed the new magazine in place. He sat with his back to the wheel and his legs stretched out in front.

If there had been eight guards to begin with, at least four were now dead and Gordi had engaged another two at the gate. That left two more, including the goon that was doing his best to kill him now. If the eighth guard turned up now, Strachey was finished. He wished, not for the first time, that Teacher had thought to include a couple of hand grenades with the other equipment.

He couldn't see where his attacker was and suspected he would soon attempt a flanking maneuver to get a better shot. Strachey was wedged between the bunker and the SUV with about two yards between them. He risked a peek over the hood and was rewarded with an immediate hail of automatic fire that thudded heavily into the engine block. One lucky shot under the car could well take off a foot, and he made himself as small a target as possible behind the wheel. The PP2000 had only a slightly slower rate of fire than the P-90, but it used a 9mm Parabellum round with superior stopping power. The situation couldn't be worse. There was furious firing back at the gate that told him that Gordi was still fully engaged. *Shit!*

Strachey fished the key to the bunker padlock out of his pocket judged the distance he would have to cover to get back to the bunker door and the time it would take to insert the key and remove the padlock. He would have a back full of 9mm slugs before he even touched the lock.

A grunt of pain reached him through his ear bud. Gordi!

"Gordi, are you ok?"

"Just took a slug in the damned leg. Can't hold them off much longer. One keeps me pinned down while the other moves in. One of the bastards is down, though."

So Gordi had been engaged by three guards. Strachey looked over his shoulder at the bunker door.

"Alberto, can you hear anything over this racket?"

"I hear you, Vop. You've got to help Gordi."

"I've got to get you out first. I'm pinned down and need another gun out here. Stand well away from the door. Go to the front corner away from door, and tell me when you've done it. Quick!"

When he received Alberto's confirmation he took careful aim at the lock and fired. The P-90's 5.7X28mm bullets could penetrate concrete, and they made quick work of the padlock and doorknob.

"You ok, Alberto?"

"Yes."

"Hold on, don't move yet."

Strachey moved carefully to the SUV's rear door and opened it, hoping the guy shooting at him thought he was still at the front of the vehicle. He reached in and grabbed the sling of one of the automatic weapons he had taken from the dead men back at the clearing and moved quickly back to the front of the SUV.

"Alberto, I'm tossing you a weapon. Maybe you can get a shot. I can't see a thing."

It was awkward to throw from a sitting position, but the PP2000 weighed only about four pounds loaded and it landed just inside the door and skittered across the floor. It was dark inside the bunker making it difficult to discern what was happening in the interior. A moment later he heard Alberto's voice.

"I've got it. I'm beside the door now. Fire a burst. If he returns fire I might see where he is."

Strachey reached his weapon over the hood again and blindly fired a long burst that was answered immediately.

"I see him," said Alberto. "He's behind a low garden wall across the drive to your left."

The next time his attacker sprayed the SUV he was met with Alberto's answering fire from the bunker door.

"Now we've got the bastard pinned down."

Strachey no longer needed the ear bud to hear Alberto.

"I'll pin him down and you move to your right to flank him."

Alberto began firing in three-shot bursts and Strachey broke cover, keeping low as he crossed the drive. The man was on his belly behind the garden wall and Strachey cut loose at him the moment he could see his body, stitching a line straight across the drive to where the man lay and struck him twice in the side. As the man tried to stand to return fire, Alberto finished him and he fell to the ground.

"Gordi!" shouted Alberto as he emerged from the bunker.

"I'll take care of Gordi."

Strachey was already running back down the drive. "You try to secure the house. There's another gun inside the SUV."

He cut through the olive grove, the sound of Gordi's firefight growing ever louder.

"Gordi, how's it going?"

"*Fantastico*. I'm bleeding like a pig and these *hijos de puta* are almost on top of me!"

Strachey came to the edge of the olive grove and crouched behind the gnarled trunk of a tree. He could see the mangled iron gates. The body of the man he had shot and run over lay in the drive and another body was not far from it. Gordi was taking fire from two men, one of whom was attempting to climb over the seven foot, stucco covered wall while the other maintained suppressing fire. The American set his fire selector to single shot and took careful aim through the MC-10-80 sight looking for a head shot and squeezed the trigger. A second later the man was dead, toppling over the wall. Strachey's weapon still had the suppressor attached which meant that the second man had not heard the shot and was unaware that he was now on his own.

"Gordi, lay down some covering fire for me."

The Spaniard's gun sounded and the second man flattened against the ground. Strachey broke cover and charged directly at him, firing from the hip as he ran, his weapon now back on full automatic. It was over in seconds, and Strachey rushed to find Gordi.

"Don't shoot, it's me. You're clear."

He found him in a ditch just outside the gates doing his best to stand on his one good leg.

"Gordi, don't move around until I can check that out."

The Spaniard sat back down at the side of the ditch with a thump.

"That guy falling over the wall scared the shit out of me!"

Gordi had taken a round in the leg that had missed the bone but taken a sizeable chunk out of his outer thigh. It was bleeding badly, but it didn't look like arterial flow to Strachey. He fished a field medical kit from the side pocket of his tactical vest and soon had a field dressing wrapped securely around Gordi's upper thigh.

It was strangely silent after the noise of battle, and Strachey wondered what was happening with Alberto in the house.

"Alberto, what's going on?"

"*Tranquilo, Vop.* Everything is under control."

It was 3:40 PM. The entire assault had lasted only ten minutes.

Strachey got Gordi to his feet and with the Spaniard's arm wrapped around his shoulder the two arrived back at the house five minutes later. Gordi noticed their rented Citroën still parked in the drive and looked reproachfully at Strachey.

"You could have fetched me in the car."

"You would just have gotten blood all over it. It's a rental, remember," grinned Strachey. Then, more seriously, "Let's get you inside so we can look after that wound properly. There must be some pain medication and antibiotic powder in the medical kit."

CHAPTER 36

When they entered the house Alberto called them to the living room where they found Fernandez, Sevillano, and the latter's wife and two children lined up on the couch with Alberto covering them with the Russian sub machinegun. The younger Fernandez was nowhere to be found.

The woman screamed and covered her eyes when she beheld the gore covering Gordi's leg, and the children took up the cry like a pack of young coyotes.

Strachey chose that moment to go out to the bullet riddled Land Rover to retrieve the duffle bags and the rest of their equipment, managing a short respite from the cacophony inside so he could update to Harvey Grant and Langley. It was another five minutes before calm was restored during which time Strachey did his best to dress Gordi's leg.

"And this was my best suit," moaned Gordi when Strachey ripped his pant leg and administered a shot of morphine from the medical kit.

Strachey gave him a quizzical look.

"Are you ever serious?"

"No," came the prompt reply.

Strachey had found the morphine ampoules in the military medical kit, and as the drug took effect, Gordi grinned evilly across the room at their prisoners.

"Hello, Director," he said cheerily. "How has your day been so far?"

Fifteen minutes later Gordi was comfortably ensconced in a large leather armchair beside the fireplace with his wounded leg, now properly bandaged, resting on a footstool.

Sevillano was in a rage.

"You'll all pay for this outrage," he blustered, "I'll see you all in prison for this! And you, Macías, will beg for prison before this is over."

Ignoring him, Alberto said to Strachey, "And this is the same fellow who wanted to have me murdered in cold blood just a few hours ago."

Alberto jerked his head toward the group on the couch and asked, "Can you see if there is someplace where Director Sevillano's wife and children can be placed -- somewhere comfortable, but with a lock on the door?"

Strachey searched the house thoroughly until he was satisfied that there was no one else there. When he came across the elaborate *Mudejar* style room Fernandez had reserved for

Muslim prayer, he whistled softly, then took some photos with his cell phone and transmitted them to Grant.

"Take a look at this, Harvey. This thing gets crazier by the minute."

"It is unexpected, but we still don't know what's really going on. By the way, Jack says to tell you well done and that he wishes he was there with you."

"I wish he was, too. We could use a few more hands. Gordi's wounded and will need some real medical attention soon."

"We know, but he'll have to wait a while longer, I'm afraid. Do you think the weapons are there?"

"I don't know, but I'll be checking on that as soon as the dust settles. You heard Fernandez admit earlier that he intended to detonate a device."

Strachey returned upstairs and then escorted Mrs. Sevillano and the children to the *Mudejar* room, which had no windows, and locked the solid oak door. Fernandez had surrendered his key ring without protest.

Thus far their "host" had said not one word in contrast with the bombastic Sevillano. He had sat tranquilly as though he had not a care in the world, a smile playing at the corners of this mouth.

Strachey didn't like it.

Leaving the group in the house, Strachey went back outside carrying a small device he had removed from one of the duffle bags and stood in the middle of the courtyard scanning the area for the best place to start. His eyes came to rest on the concrete bunker where Alberto had been imprisoned, its door still hanging half open. Beside it was a large generator unit with tall exhaust stacks.

He walked over for a closer look. The bunker was windowless, and the door was much larger than would be required for just a person to enter. Measuring about 12 X 12 feet, the interior was festooned with electrical and refrigeration connections and a control box was appended to one wall. There were two empty cradles that could have held large, cylindrical shapes. Strachey pushed a button on the device in his hands and a color LCD panel on its front lit up. He pushed another button and the screen displayed a series of red bars, similar to the signal strength display on a cell phone. At the same time it emitted a steady beep.

He stepped back out through the door and the beeping decreased in frequency as the display retreated from three bars to one.

"Harvey," he said into the cell phone. "We've got residual radioactivity inside the bunker. It's big enough for two devices to have been stored there, and the power and refrigeration couplings could have served to maintain them the same as they would have been in a Russian weapons depot. If I don't miss my guess, this bunker was constructed specifically for that purpose. Unfortunately, it's empty now."

"The residual radioactivity is more confirmation that he actually possesses the Russian landmines," said Grant. "At every step of the way the evidence has grown stronger. Now we have Fernandez's admission earlier today to Macías and confirmation that nuclear materials were recently stored at the compound. I'm afraid we don't have much time left to set the alternative plan in motion."

Strachey looked at his watch. It was five P.M. Tomorrow would be Christmas Day.

"I know, Harvey. Please keep a look out for us and let me know if it looks like visitors. I have some cleaning up to do now."

He found a pick-up truck in the barn with the keys in the ignition and drove back toward the entrance. Thirty minutes later he returned the truck to its space in the garage. Its bed now contained five bodies, two from the clearing across the river and three from the gate area. He then dragged the other two dead guards from the courtyard into the barn and slid the doors closed. With some effort he had managed also to push the wrought iron gates at the entrance back into some semblance of their original position. It was grisly work. He had no love for the men, but he treated their bodies with respect. There had been no joy in the killing.

He removed his tactical and bullet proof vest, but he was now covered with blood that had leaked from the bodies when he moved them.

He turned away from the barn and walked back into the house.

CHAPTER 37

Sevillano was still fulminating beside a tranquil Fernandez on the couch when Strachey returned. His gruesome task had put him on edge and he walked over to stand in front of the police Director, where he removed his pistol from its holster and pointed it directly at Sevillano's forehead.

"Shut up, now, and don't speak again unless asked to do so, you *comemierda* shit eating bastard."

Sevillano opened his mouth to reply then thought better of it and his jaws snapped shut with a click.

Strachey retrieved his civilian clothing from a duffle bag and stalked out of the room to change, leaving total silence in his wake.

When he returned he found that Alberto had pulled a chair up to sit facing their prisoners, and he followed suit.

Alberto was saying, "Sr. Fernandez, earlier

today you admitted to me that you intend to detonate a nuclear device somewhere in Spain. Tell me where."

Fernandez regarded the Spanish policeman with cool, appraising eyes.

Finally, he said, "I misjudged you, *Comisario* Macías. Of all people, I should have known better, but killing you would have served no purpose because it would have made no difference."

Waving a careless hand, he continued, "Just as nothing you have done here today will make any difference. You are far too late. *'The moving finger writes; and having writ, moves on: nor all your piety nor wit shall lure it back to cancel half a line, nor all your tears wash out a word of it.'* Omar Khayyam stated the futility of wishing history could be re-written quite wonderfully, don't you think?"

"We need you to tell us where you've set the bombs," persisted Alberto.

"Oh, only one has been set. Its purpose is to serve as proof of our seriousness and to demonstrate that we will detonate the second if our demands are not met."

"You'll kill tens of thousands of innocent people."

"Yes, and it will give me no pleasure, but even that will be a small price for Spain to pay for its crimes against our people."

"Crimes?"

"Of course. I asked you earlier, *Comisario,*

if you were a student of history. Even a poorly educated Spaniard must be dimly aware of the terrible crimes of the *Reconquista*, of the genocidal methods of your ancestors, the mass expulsion of innocent people – entire families, many tens of thousands – the greedy confiscation of their property, the atrocities committed by the Inquisition, only because they subscribed to their own faith. Muslims and Jews were wantonly massacred, ripped from the land they had known for nearly a thousand years." His voice trembled now with emotion. "I asked you before, *Comisario*, what you thought of ethnic cleansing. It's a crime against humanity, is it not? What was the 'cleansing' of Spain, the destruction of *Al Andaluz*, if not ethnic cleansing? My people shall have their revenge, and we shall recover what is by rights ours."

"What are you talking about? Who are 'your people'?"

Fernandez's words made no sense.

"I am Muhammad XIV," said Fernandez with a flourish and a lift of his chin. He sat up straight, "Caliph of *Al Andaluz.*"

He looked around the room expectantly, but saw only consternation in the faces of his captors.

"He's truly insane," said Strachey, staring at Fernandez, "a complete loon."

"You will not speak that way to the Sultan," hissed Sevillano. "By this time tomorrow, you will crawl on your bellies to him and beg for his mercy."

"I thought I told you to shut up," returned Strachey.

Fernandez placed a restraining hand on Sevillano's arm.

"Remain calm, my friend. Our time will come soon enough."

He addressed Strachey.

"I assume your superiors are aware of your presence here?" He now spoke in unaccented English.

"Yes, they are."

Strachey didn't reveal that a select group of CIA officers was listening live, via Grant's satellite hook up with Langley, to everything that was being said.

"I have nothing against the Americans," said Fernandez, "although I deplore the corruption and immorality of your society. My fight is only with Spain, and my cause is just."

He checked the gold Vacherin Constantine watch on his wrist.

"In just a few hours, at midnight tonight, Spain will be changed forever. The entire world will be changed. As I said, there is nothing you can do to prevent it."

Strachey was jolted, and he could see that Alberto was likewise. It was nearing seven P.M. They had only five hours left.

Fernandez was still talking.

"And when the first bomb has demonstrated our seriousness, we shall make our demands known to the public: the return of our land, of *Al*

Andaluz, to its rightful heir and ruler," he paused dramatically and placed a hand over his heart, "the direct descendant of Abu Abdullah, whom you know as Boabdil, and we shall rebuild our wonderful Caliphate, and it shall be as a light unto Islam!"

This guy is totally delusional, thought Strachey.

"Bob," Grant's voice sounded in his ear, "we got all of that, and Langley's recorded everything from the start. We know he has a bomb and now we know what time it's supposed to detonate, but we still don't know where."

No one was more aware that time was running out that Strachey. Even now, even if the Spanish authorities were notified, they could never mobilize in time. An entire city could not be searched and its population evacuated in a just few hours. There was only one way to prevent disaster.

Standing, he said, "We don't have any more time, Fernandez. Either tell us where the device is hidden or we'll have to resort to more direct methods of interrogation."

Fernandez looked up at him, his eyes unafraid.

"You may try, but it will gain you nothing. Even I do not know precisely where the weapon has been placed within the city we selected. We planned it thus in case of an eventuality such as this. Torturing me or my friend here will do you no good. And should we have to die, we will do so gladly. We are not alone. The other members of the *Hermandad*, our brotherhood, are safe in North Africa awaiting the moment for their triumphal return, and if I am gone, my son, Miguel, will take my place."

"How can you possibly believe that such a mad scheme would work? You could never hope to hold the territory you claim."

"You underestimate us. We have powerful allies who will lend their military strength to our cause, who will send their soldiers and their weapons, and who will threaten an even greater nuclear holocaust if we are attacked."

"The Iranians," said Alberto.

"Quite perceptive," said Fernandez. "And if you know anything about my Persian allies, you know they would welcome nothing more than Armageddon."

"Yeah," said Strachey in disgust, "they're as nuts as you." He stood then and unholstered his pistol. "Let's see just how nuts you really are."

He snapped the pistol up and without hesitating shot Sevillano in the knee. The armor piercing round made a small hole when it entered, easily traversed the bone and left a nasty exit wound in the back of the police Director's leg. His howl was worthy of a lovesick cat as he reacted in sudden pain and surprise and grabbed his leg.

Desperate times call for desperate measures, thought Strachey, and he suspected that Sevillano's devotion to the cause was not as great as his master's.

"That was to show you I'm serious and also because I really don't like you," he said, bending low so his face was only inches from Sevillano's.

With a yelp of horror, Fernandez had shot to his feet to put distance between himself and the bleeding and moaning Sevillano.

Alberto, too, was shocked by the suddenness and the violence of Strachey's action, and Gordi sat upright in his chair with his standard exclamation, "*Joder!!*"

Strachey turned his attention back to Fernandez who was gaping at his now gray-faced comrade and the crimson stain that was spreading across the expensive couch behind his wounded leg.

"Now you will tell us the location of the device," rasped Strachey, "or it'll be your turn, only with you I'll start with the ankles and work my way up."

Fernandez was clearly shaken, more fearful that Sevillano would talk than of his own safety.

"I already told you it would do no good. Nothing can stop it now, and if I am unable to communicate my demands to the President of Spain tomorrow, the second bomb will be detonated, and it's already in Madrid."

"You can still talk without the use of your legs," said Strachey.

CHAPTER 38

There was a pounding in his ears and it was a moment before Strachey realized that Grant was yelling at him through the ear bud.

"Bob! What the hell's going on? We heard a gunshot."

"Director Sevillano had an accident," said Strachey. "We're out of time. This bastard's going to talk."

"Hold on, Bob. Amy Dawson just picked up something with Palantir that you may be able to use.

It was nearing two in the afternoon in Virginia, and Amy had returned to her console that morning after two hours' sleep and a quick shower. Now she directed Palantir's powerful search engine through the ether in a quest for clues, anything that might add to their knowledge. Her efforts had been rewarded ten minutes earlier when an electronic ping alerted her that she had a hit. She'd related the information to Teacher as soon as she had a read-out.

Grant's voice was excited, and Strachey listened intently as he continued.

"Amy says that someone using Zarin's French alias purchased a plane ticket to fly from León to Madrid. The same credit card was used for a ticket for a second man. They left on the seven P.M. flight today and should be landing in Madrid about now."

With an effort, Strachey kept the emotion from his face as Grant fed him Amy's information.

"Wait just a second," he said.

He wondered if Fernandez played poker.

Holstering his pistol, he ordered Fernandez to sit back down.

"I don't think we need anything more from you. The matter is being taken care of."

A puzzled expression appeared on Fernandez's face.

"What do you mean?"

Strachey deadpanned, "We know all about León."

Fernandez's jaw dropped. "H-how...?" His voice trailed off.

That reaction was all the confirmation Strachey needed. He spoke to Grant.

"That's it, Harvey. It's as good as we're going to get."

"We'll get things underway from our end."

"Right, oh, and by the way, Harvey..."

"Yes?"

"Tell Teacher he'd damned well better make certain that Amy gets a promotion and a bonus."

"You bet."

"And tell Nico to have the LearJet prepped for a quick departure sometime after midnight."

Strachey vowed to take Amy to the best dinner Washington had to offer the next time he was in town.

It was 8:30 P.M.

*****

Jack Teacher picked up a secure line and dialed the White House the moment he was off the sat phone with Grant. He spoke for fifteen minutes with the President of the United States.

*****

At nine o'clock in the evening the gala Christmas Eve dinner and dance was well underway at the Moncloa Palace when a uniformed military steward slipped into the ballroom and sidled silently up to the Spanish President who was engaged in conversation with a group of Madrid notables.

The steward whispered into the President's ear evoking a pained expression. Clearly annoyed at the interruption, he offered his excuses to the group and followed the steward out of the ballroom and back to the business side of the building to his office. What could the President of the United States be calling him about now? Surely not the same nonsense as this morning. The Americans had become alarmists.

He moved around to sit behind the antique desk that had once belonged to Alfonso XIII and warily eyed the blinking light on the secure telephone. With a sigh, he raised the receiver.

"Mr. President," he said in his very good English, "Merry Christmas. To what do I owe the honor?"

As he listened to the well-known, persuasive voice speaking to him from Washington, his face turned ashen.

The voice ceased and the President sat very still for several seconds as he fought to control the panic that was rising from his gut.

"It's confirmed?" he asked, and listened to the answer, feeling panic give way to desperation as the urgency of the situation was finally brought home.

"But it's surely too late to do anything, and what you ask is unprecedented..."

The voice from Washington interrupted to tell him he had the choice between being known as the man who had been forewarned and still knowingly permitted a Spanish city to be destroyed or the man who did his best to prevent it.

"What do you want me to do?" he asked.

*****

Strachey had finally removed the ear bud as they waited for developments. He had dressed Sevillano's knee, and that worthy had been locked into the *Mudejar* room where his wife could attend to him and listen to his whining.

They kept Fernandez in the living room with them. He had finally begun to speak again. In a dreamy voice he recited the historical injustices committed by the Spanish Crown and the Catholic Church, the travails of the *moriscos* and *maranos* over the centuries, the forced expulsion of entire populations. And he praised the glories of *Al Andaluz.*

They were fascinated despite themselves as he described the history of his family. It was all like something from *The Arabian Nights*, or Washington Irving's *Tales of the Alhambra.* Alberto was incredulous when he told them of a Spaniard, Eduardo Macías, improbably one of Alberto's ancestors, and his battle with the inquisitor of Seville, but Fernandez assured him it was all true. "It's why you are still alive, *Comisario*, my family owes yours a debt of gratitude.[3] Doesn't your family still possess an old dagger, perhaps, in the Moorish style?"

Alberto had not made the connection during

---

[3] See THE INQUISITOR AND THE MAIDEN, Michael R. Davidson, 2013.

Fernandez's recitation, but he now felt a shock of recognition as his thoughts flew to his apartment in Madrid to the shelf in his living room where the time worn dagger with its battered brass sheath lay – his son David's favorite object that he had found in his grandparents' attic in Sepúlveda.

He pulled himself to his feet and crossed the room to the stone fireplace where he took down the antique rapier that was identical to the one that, according to Fernandez, his ancestor had wielded. Bemused, Alberto grasped the sword and flicked his wrist, causing the still sharp narrow blade to whistle in the air. Somehow, it felt right in his hand.

He turned to see Fernandez watching him and despite the monstrous plot the man had conceived, pity welled up within him. How had such an honorable past become so perverted and come to such an ignominious end?

His charitable mood was broken when Fernandez's eyes hardened and he said, "I don't know how you found out about León, but it makes no difference. There is no time for you to find the bomb ... and then there is the one in Madrid. If *Al Andaluz* is not conceded to me, then both cities will be annihilated and nobody wins."

*****

It was nearly 10:30 P.M. before the first police units arrived at the Fernandez compound. They heard the helicopter coming in low over the courtyard outside, and by the time Alberto opened the door, the GEO unit was already rappelling down the ropes from the hovering chopper.

Alberto identified himself and was pleasantly surprised when the GE0 Commander saluted and said, "Yes, *Comisario*, we know who you are and our instructions are to follow your orders to the letter."

Alberto's face must have betrayed his astonishment because the Commander continued immediately, "Those instructions came directly from the Office of the President."

Now that's a real surprise! I wonder what finally got the bastard off his Socialist ass. The *Comisario Principal* briefed the GEO commandos on what they would find inside the house and about the bodies they would find in the barn. The Commander ordered some of his men to take up guard positions around the house while the others searched the rest of the property. He would personally take charge of the prisoner, Ricardo Sevillano. A medical team, he said was already on its way.

Alberto was thinking fast. According to Fernandez, the second bomb was already in Madrid and the *Comisario* did not intend to sit in Aznalcazar and wait for someone else to find it. He went inside to consult with Strachey and Gordi, and a half-hour later Alberto and the CIA man were aboard the GE0 chopper flying back eastward towards Seville. Beside them sat a shackled Miguel Fernandez. Gordi, who had objected strenuously to being left behind, was on his way to a local hospital so his leg could be properly looked after.

The chopper put them down on the tarmac near Nico's LearJet and the two hustled Fernandez up the boarding stairs to find Grant and Nico waiting for them. Nico headed for the cockpit and soon had the engines spinning as they strapped Fernandez into a seat. Grant informed them that Spanish airspace had been closed until further notice but thanks to a personal request from the President of the United States to the President of Spain, theirs would be one of very few aircraft still permitted in the sky that evening.

CHAPTER 39

The Iberia domestic flight carrying Zarin and Shirazi from León touched down in Madrid shortly before 8:00 P.M., a few minutes ahead of schedule, and Zarin hustled his companion through the terminal and outside to the taxi queue. The Colonel intended to be inside the Iranian Embassy well before the fireworks started in León. He gave the address to the driver and settled back into the seat with a satisfied sigh.

Turning his head so he could see Shirazi's profile, he said in Farsi, "Now we wait. We have nine days before your next job."

He thought it had been clever of Fernandez to have selected January 3, the anniversary of Abu Abdullah's exile from Granada, as the target date for the second bomb. In the meantime he could envision the rampant chaos that was about to grip the country as people fleeing the cities clogged the highways and public transport. Emergency services would be stretched beyond the breaking point in a vain attempt to deal with the aftermath of the nuclear blast in León. In all likelihood all flights would be grounded, and the government would make a futile effort to quarantine the population to clear the roadways for emergency and security services while the central government wrestled with Fernandez's ultimatum.

Zarin believed the weak Spanish government might quickly capitulate. After all, the entire population had crumbled to the demands of Al Qaeda after the bombings in 2004. Those had been mere conventional explosives. What would they do when faced with nuclear blackmail? He didn't believe the crisis would ever come to the point of actually detonating the second device.

The Spanish government would have no choice but to allow the evacuation of Embassy staffs, and there was a diplomatic passport waiting for him that would guarantee his safe passage. The blond Iranian swelled with pride as he imagined the impending success of his mission. He would be received in Tehran as a hero. Perhaps they would send him back to Spain to head the Iranian contingent in the new *Andaluz* where he would quickly disabuse that old fool Fernandez of the idea that he had any real power in the face of the Islamic Republic's might.

After the taxi deposited them at the embassy, Zarin pressed the call button at the gate, and a guard arrived in quick order to check their identities and let them in.

"Come with me," he said to Shirazi, and led him around the building to the parking area. Waiting for them was the truck that Shirazi had noticed when they were leaving two days earlier, a truck identical to the one they'd left in Léon. Standing beside it was a man cut from the same cloth as the guards he had seen at Fernandez's place. The second bomb had been waiting here in the embassy compound since before Zarin had paid his surprise visit, a place the Spanish authorities had no right to search.

"You see, Shirazi, we have thought of everything." And the Colonel laughed.

CHAPTER 40

At precisely 11:20 P.M. on Christmas Eve a bright light appeared high in the sky over ancient León, followed a second later by the clap and roar of a tremendous explosion.

*****

Some thirty minutes earlier, 300 miles on a bearing due west from Oporto on the Portuguese coast the deck of the nuclear aircraft carrier CVN 75, the USS Harry S. Truman, had tilted to the rear of the F/A 18F Super Hornet as its pilot, Commander Gary Cooper, banked sharply to the east and streaked away from the Second Fleet's carrier task group. The twin rudders of the dual seat multirole fighter were painted dark blue with yellow trim and the outline of a yellow sword slanting to the rear, showing that the plane belonged to Strike Fighter Squadron Three Two, nicknamed the "Swordsmen." The same markings adorned the tail of Cooper's wingman off his port wing.

Cooper's "wizzo," Larry Cramer, his weapons systems officer, began bringing his systems on-line for the task ahead as Cooper kicked the GE F414 turbofan engines and the Super Hornet soared to altitude at 40,000 feet. Once at altitude he pushed the plane to just above Mach 1, considerably below the aircraft's Mach 1.8 maximum speed due to the drag created by the fuel tank mounted on a pylon under his left wing and a single satellite-guided joint directed attack munition, or JDAM, mounted on a pylon under the right wing.

Less than fifteen minutes later, the Portuguese coastline came into view and they powered down as they adjusted course to their target 200 miles to the northeast. Behind the two U.S. Naval warplanes, the Harry S. Truman Carrier Strike Group (HSTCSG) surged eastward at flank speed to close the distance the F/A 18'S would have to remain airborne on their trip back as they would be at the edge of their operational range. On the direct orders of the President of the United States the carrier strike group, a part of the U.S. Second Fleet in the Atlantic, had been steaming toward the Iberian Peninsula since the day before. To the south, the U.S. Sixth Fleet's carrier strike group in the Mediterranean had likewise been placed on alert. The designation of León, Spain, as the target meant the task would fall to the air wing of the Second Fleet's CVN 75.

Dropping below the speed of sound as they approached to within one hundred miles of their target Cramer made the last of his adjustments to the JDAM's GPS controlled guidance system and prepared for a "slingshot" launch. The escort fighter remained at 40,000 feet and began to circle the target area to defend against any possible intrusion while Cooper jettisoned the now empty extra fuel tank and descended below the toss altitude that would guarantee optimal deployment of the JDAM and then drove the plane's nose back up to regain 25,000 feet. The "wizzo" released the "drop and forget" weapon when they were still 15 miles from the target site and Cooper pulled the Super Hornet into a tight 180 degree turn and kicked in the afterburners to escape the target area. His wing man rejoined him and both planes streaked back toward the Atlantic Coast and a rendezvous with the fleet.

The JDAM's warhead carried one of the most sophisticated weapons in the secret arsenal of the United States – a directed energy weapon. An earlier, still experimental version of such a weapon had been used at the start of the Persian Gulf War, when the U.S. Navy had dropped electromagnetic pulse warheads on Baghdad to disrupt centralized military command and control systems and weapons systems, such as anti-aircraft missile sites. As a result the Iraqi central command had been left with no way to coordinate military units and their Soviet made anti-aircraft missiles had to be fired blind into the night sky.

Since then the design and effective radius of the High-power microwave (HPM) E-bomb had been dramatically enhanced as had the minimization of collateral damage that normally would be caused by the conventional explosion that triggered the HPM pulse. In fact, the electronics portion of the particular bomb just launched by Commander Cooper's F/A 18F comprised fully 85% of its total mass, and it would have a "kill radius" of one mile, a capability unheard of just a few years earlier for non-nuclear devices. This weapon would emit extremely short pulse wave forms in the millimetric microwave bands that would fry even shielded electrical circuits and disable equipment across its effective radius.

The JDAM's precise GPS guidance system took it silently through the dark sky on an arced trajectory that would bring it perpendicular, it's nose pointed directly at the ground, at a point one mile above the center of León where the explosives would detonate, the maximum height that could achieve a high-power microwave pulse that would be of sufficient "lethality" to cover the designated target area when it reached the ground nanoseconds after the blast. The mission planners had calculated that a circle two miles wide would encompass the area most likely to have been chosen for placement of the 10-kiloton nuclear weapon if the terrorists were aiming for maximum devastation. The planners had been especially concerned about the Hospital San Juan de Dios that lay just outside the circle of destruction. The hospital, they knew, would be needed before the night was over, and there would be some spill-over effects of the magnetic pulse well beyond the kill zone.

And so, at precisely 11:20 P.M. on Christmas Eve a bright light appeared high in the sky over ancient León, followed a second later by the clap of a loud explosion that shattered windows in those structures nearest the epicenter, but while there was inevitable blast damage, the new composite casing of the JDAM had been designed to minimize shrapnel, and the bomb's vertical position at detonation would scatter the light casing fragments that had not been consumed in the blast laterally dispersing them over a wide area so as to minimize damage.

Lights went out, the few cars still on the streets stopped dead with fused ignition systems. Computers died, and Christmas tree lights blinked out. Unfortunately for some, pacemakers also stopped working. It would be months before the city could return to normal. Hundreds of millions of dollars in damages were inflicted, but in the parking lot at the rear of the *Parador San Marcos*, the short pulse wave penetrated the shielding to the electrical circuitry inside the gray metal shell of the Russian nuclear landmine and rendered it incapable of detonation. The city, though severely crippled, would still be there on Christmas morning. Had there been a 10-kiloton nuclear event, much of it would have been vaporized and the rest converted to rubble by the shockwave. The monetary and human costs would have been almost beyond the Spanish Government's capabilities.

An hour earlier the President of Spain had called a national defense alert, the first in the nation's history since the Civil War in the Thirties, and emergency vehicles were speeding toward León already.

CHAPTER 41

They landed at Barajas International Airport at about the same time the HPM bomb was being slingshotted above León. Grant had brought up the naval commo frequency via the secure data link with Langley, and they all remained on board after Nico had shut down the engines to await confirmation that the weapon was on its way. The pilot of the F/A18 confirmed that the JDAM had detonated over the target.

As soon as they had confirmed that León was the target Grant had suggested that the KH-11 surveillance satellite be repositioned to cover the city, and they too could see the flash as the bomb exploded. The city went dark almost immediately.

Now all they could do was wait to find out if the nuclear device had indeed been deactivated by the microwave pulse, so they remained aboard the LearJet crowded around Grant's computer.

Midnight came and passed with no blinding flash from a nuclear explosion, but still they waited and watched. Despite himself, Fernandez, still shackled in his seat, could not contain his curiosity. He did not understand what was happening, but he knew what time it was and he didn't like the fact that his captors were showing no signs of grief.

By 12:30 A.M. they were breathing more easily, and Alberto said to the prisoner, "León is still in one piece, Sr. Fernandez. Your plan has failed."

The self-styled "caliph" was disappointed but not distraught. "Perhaps you are telling the truth, *Comisario*, perhaps not, but as I told you before, it really makes no difference. Both you and the Spanish Government have confirmed that I was serious and possessed the means to destroy one of your cities. So even if you did manage to stop the operation in León, the result is the same. The Government realizes that the threat is real, that there is a second device already in Madrid, and my demands are unchanged. If they are not met, then Madrid will be destroyed. I order you to take me to see the President."

"I suspect that the President is too busy right now to see you, Sr. Fernandez. But you're at least partially correct: he will now see that the threat was real … is real, and that real action is required."

Fernandez held his chin high.

"And when the Spanish people hear my ultimatum, they will force him to capitulate. They will have no stomach for resistance." He closed his eyes as though he were envisioning a resurrected *Al Andaluz*. "We shall have our just revenge, and our lands shall be returned to us."

"He's a hopeless case, Alberto," said Strachey, observing the obstinate confidence of their captive. "What do you want to do now?"

They Spaniard thought hard. They were still playing by ear rather than reading from Fernandez's sheet music.

"What happens," he asked Fernandez, "if no one hears anything from you, no ultimatum, nothing?"

Fernandez settled against his seatback and eyed the Spanish cop.

"Then, my dear Macías, the second bomb goes 'boom.'"

"When?"

"You want a deadline? I'll be happy to provide one. If I am permitted to issue my ultimatum publicly, via all national and international media, your government will have nine days to make its decision, until January 3 to be precise. That is a very significant date, you know."

"Enlighten us," put in Strachey.

"On January 3, 1492 my ancestor, Abu Abdullah who you might know as Boabdil, was exiled from his beloved Granada by King Fernando and Queen Isabella. It would be quite poetic if the Spanish now were to relinquish it to me on the anniversary, don't you think?"

Strachey translated this for Grant and the team listening in back at Langley, and now the ever cautious Grant said, "We need to think through the ramifications of allowing him to make a public statement. It would have an effect far beyond the borders of Spain. In fact, do we even want the public ever to know that a nuclear device actually fell into the hands of terrorists and that they were able to arm it and threaten the integrity of a European nation? The decision is far above the pay grade of anyone on this plane, and like it or not we have to turn it over to the politicians now."

When Strachey translated this for Alberto, the latter reluctantly nodded his head in agreement. Their team had done all they could do, and they had succeeded spectacularly, but they both realized that the time for making their own rules had come to an end. In reality, their power to affect events had been limited from the start: all they could do was uncover facts that would empower elected officials to act. León had been spared annihilation because the President of the United States had believed their intelligence and acted upon it. Neither Strachey nor Grant nor even the Director of Central Intelligence could have ordered the U.S. Navy to drop the HMP bomb or convince the Spanish president that such action was necessary.

Strachey jerked his head toward Fernandez.

"What do we do with him?"

Alberto had to think about this because he didn't want to relinquish physical control of Fernandez just yet. If he took him to the offices of the Secretary of State for Security or the Ministry of the Interior certain decisions would be taken completely out of his hands as the legal machinery of State creaked fitfully, probably hysterically, into motion. And he was mindful of the duplicity of Director of the National Police Ricardo Sevillano. Could there be others like him in high government positions? The thought of Strachey shooting Sevillano flashed through his mind. Grant had been right – the strategic decisions were out of their hands, but critical tactical decisions might still have to be made. The GEO Commander had said that Alberto was in charge, and he saw no reason to change that now.

"Let's take him to Canillas," he said.

Canillas, a neighborhood in northeastern Madrid, was the location of the *Comisaría General de Información*, the Directorate of Intelligence, of the National Police, where all counter-terrorist activities were coordinated. Alberto had good friends there, especially the Director, Gabriel Fonseca.

A police van and car were waiting beside the LearJet when they at last debarked, and a uniformed officer jumped out to greet Alberto, who told him where he wanted to go. He bundled the still handcuffed Fernandez into the back of the car and slid in beside him. Strachey and Grant clambered into the van, leaving Nico to put his jet to bed, and the motorcade covered the short distance to their destination in ten minutes.

The Directorate of Intelligence was housed in a low, reinforced concrete building with few windows that was surrounded by a high security wall. Once inside, Alberto led them confidently to the basement where they discovered a lounge, complete with knotty pine walls, several beer taps, and a couple of shelves of the stronger stuff behind the bar. Ranged around the sides of the room were comfortably padded benches and tables. The Spanish version of a coffee break room.

Leaving Fernandez in the care of Strachey and Grant, Alberto climbed the stairs to the first floor where he found Gabriel Fonseca in his office. It seemed everyone had been called back from leave.

Gabriel, a tall phlegmatic man several years younger than Alberto, raised his bespectacled eyes from the papers on his desk as his door opened. "I might have known you would be involved in this," he said and rose to step around the desk and give Alberto a bear hug. "I heard what you and your friends did down south. How is Gordi?"

"He'll be fine. He pissed and moaned about being left behind, but the medic said he needed a hospital and that he shouldn't be flying in his condition anyway. Can I use your secure phone?"

"Sure, be my guest. And sit down for Heaven's sake. You look like the walking dead!"

Alberto sank gratefully into Gabriel's desk chair and dialed the Moncloa Palace. He identified himself to the switchboard and was mildly surprised to be put through directly to President Camisero whom he filled in on the events in Aznalcazar. The President already had been informed of Sevillano's treachery, but he sucked in his breath sharply when Alberto described the way the police Director had wanted to have him killed. The nationality of the guards at Fernandez' compound combined with the identification of Zarin and Shirazi added a serious international complication to the situation Spain now confronted.

When the details of Fernandez's demands and his ultimatum were described there was a long silence at the other end of the line. Alberto could only imagine the effect his words were having on President Camisero and for the first time he felt pity for the man.

The Spanish President's next words when finally they came were entirely unexpected.

"What is your advice, *Comisario*?"

With a glance at Gabriel, he replied, "I think you should continue to consult with the American president. Mr. Grant believes there are many as yet undetermined ramifications to be considered. Then you'll have to decide."

Camisero's voice was soft when he spoke.

"You're right, Macías. You were right all along and I apologize for not taking you seriously. What about this fellow, Fernandez?"

"Thank you for that, *Sr. Presidente*. I have Fernandez here with me at Canillas. I recommend we keep him here while we sort things out. In the meantime I'd like to call in all the GEO personnel that are available, and TEDAX, as well."

"The TEDAX NRBQ unit is already in Leon and GEO is standing by for orders," said Camisero.

"We'll need TEDAX back in Madrid as soon as they've finished there."

"As you wish, *Comisario*, and thank you again."

TEDAX NRBQ is the CNP's explosives detection and deactivation unit that specializes in nuclear, radiological, biological, and chemical weapons disposal. It's the Spanish version of America's N.E.S.T., the Department of Energy's Nuclear Emergency Support Team although its numbers do not begin to match the more than 1,000 members of N.E.S.T.

When the connection was broken Alberto filled Gabriel in on what President Camisero had said.

"I'm going to suggest that Grant get on the phone with Langley and brief them. We can use any good ideas they can come up with, and I hope their president will stay in touch with Camisero."

"No doubt about that," said Gabriel, "right now, there's no more pressing problem anywhere on earth."

When he returned downstairs he filled the Americans in on what Camisero had said and suggested that Grant call Langley.

Using his secure cell phone, Grant dialed the number and began talking.

CHAPTER 42

Miguel Fernandez followed the talk flowing around him and about him with undisguised interest. *So far, so good,* he thought, but he was worried about the influence the Americans were having. He had to force the Spanish to play by his rules.

"You didn't let me finish my answer," he said quietly.

"What are you talking about now," asked Alberto.

"You asked what would happen if I did not issue a public ultimatum."

"Yes, and you said the bomb would be set off on January 3."

"You don't remember what I told you earlier? January 3 is the deadline I will give in the ultimatum. If nothing is heard from me at all, I gave orders that the device should be detonated at noon on Christmas Day – and I think that is today."

*****

The military transport, a C-130 with Spanish Air Force markings, carrying the TEDAX NRBQ unit landed at the León airport, located well away from the city, shortly after midnight. They were well-trained and well-equipped, and they quickly released two of their specially equipped vans from their restraints in the cargo hold and soon had them on the tarmac. The radiation detection vehicle that TEDAX had pre-positioned in Leon would have been rendered inoperable by the HMP pulse. Paco Mendoza, who was in command of the unit, had been thinking hard during the short flight, and he had a plan.

Logically, to gain maximum effect from a ground burst, a nuclear device would have to be emplaced in the open. He assumed that the device which had been described to him weighed some five tons, that it would have to have been transported in at least a medium sized truck, and the terrorists would have wanted to park it outside. At the same time, they would have wanted it to be somewhere in or near the city center and that would have limited their options.

As they approached the darkened city Mendoza held a flashlight to illuminate the city map on his knees. There were few open public parking areas in the crowded center of town and his attention was captured by the large open areas surrounding the *Parador San Marcos* and the Provincial Government building. He followed his instincts and ordered his driver to take them there first.

His five-man team fanned out through the parking area that lay between the Provincial Government building and the huge, rambling structure of the Parador and also the hotel parking lot in the rear. Each of them wore a backpack that carried the detection equipment

Within twenty minutes one of his men had spotted the truck with the canvas covered cargo area parked in a corner of the hotel lot, and their Geiger counters detected definite radiation. When they gingerly pulled back the rear flap of the truck's cargo area the sight of the squat gray cylinder made them gasp.

*****

In Madrid, Alberto informed the group that TEDAX had located the Russian nuclear landmine and disconnected the trigger mechanism. It may have been fried, but they were taking no chances. The device had been transferred to a truck commandeered from the local airport and was on its way back to Madrid under police guard. The Guardia Civil had closed all roads to normal traffic.

Grant had been on a conference call with the group and Langley and the White House, where the President had assembled his Cabinet.

Given the six-hour time difference, it was still Christmas Eve in Washington.

They had no way of knowing the truth of Fernandez's claim that the Madrid device would be detonated at noon if his ultimatum were not made public, but to permit the world to learn that nuclear weapons were in the hands of terrorists and that they were blackmailing an entire nation was unappetizing. To do so would gain time during which the Spanish could try to find the hidden weapon and disarm it, but it would also encourage the emulation of other terrorist groups and induce widespread panic. It could well encourage western countries, especially certain countries in Europe, to seek accommodation with the terrorists and their sponsors, leaving the United States even more isolated than it was already.

The Spanish were willing to listen to American advice, but at the end of the day the final decision was theirs and theirs alone. Practically speaking, there was nothing America could do now beyond offer support. Dropping another HMP weapon on Madrid was not an option because a bomb capable of generating a pulse strong enough to black out the entire city of over three million inhabitants would have to be powered by a nuclear air burst and no one in Washington or Madrid was willing even to contemplate such an eventuality.

The result was inevitable: the Spanish Government would hold out as long as possible, until eleven A.M. while every effort was made to discover the location of the second bomb. If it remained undiscovered by then, Fernandez would be allowed to issue his ultimatum via the public media.

By the time all this had been discussed and agreed between the American and Spanish presidents, it was three A.M. in Madrid.

Only eight hours remained to find the bomb.

CHAPTER 43

Paco Mendoza and his team were ordered to fly immediately back to Madrid and by 4:30 A.M. the five TEDAX NRBQ vans, equipped with sophisticated radiation detection gear were patrolling the streets of Madrid and an American surveillance satellite had been positioned over the city.

If the ultimatum were issued panic instantly would grip the terrorized population of the great city and, travel restrictions or not, there would be a mass rush for the exit. Streets and roadways would be clogged as over three million inhabitants sought to escape. People inevitably would die in the ensuing melee, and similar panic would grip other cities in the country. Maintaining public order would be impossible.

Six and a half hours now remained.

*****

Alberto instructed that Fernandez be placed in a holding cell on the building's main level. He was weary of the increasingly insufferable man's company and just didn't want to be near him for a while. Hopefully, no one in the government would think to ask for him before 11:00 A.M. rolled around because Alberto was thinking seriously about some enhanced interrogation techniques, and he didn't care about leaving marks. He was sure that no one in this building, at least, would object.

Alberto sat on a stool at the bar rubbing his tired eyes with his knuckles. He realized that exactly twenty-four hours had passed since he had driven to the Moncloa with Ricardo Sevillano for the disastrous meeting with the President the previous morning. Aside from a couple of catnaps while they were airborne, he had not slept and he now found it hard to believe that so much had happened in so little time. He forced himself to ignore the fatigue and keep his mind focused.

After a few moments, he climbed the stairs to consult again with Gabriel Fonseca, and when he returned to the group he switched on the espresso machine behind the bar, loaded it with freshly ground beans, and it soon produced two double doses of strong, black Spanish coffee. When it was ready he called Strachey over.

Passing a steaming cup to the American,

Alberto said, "I've been thinking. We know what flight Zarin and Shirazi brought back to Madrid and what time it landed. They had to go to ground somewhere, and someone may have been waiting to pick them up. It's also possible that Zarin may not believe we have the alias he was using and rented another car, or they might have taken a taxi. I just asked Gabi Fonseca to check with the car rental agencies and canvas the cab drivers that were on duty last night? There shouldn't be a lot of them, given that it was Christmas Eve."

"Good idea."

Strachey had been thinking along the same lines and reported that Amy Dawson already was using Palantir to check the car rental records.

"And I have a hunch of my own," Strachey continued. "It may be a shortcut to what we're after, but we'll need to pull one of the TEDAX trucks away from wherever it is now."

The radiation detection vans were following carefully planned routes around the city according to a grid pattern that was designed to allow them to cover the maximum area in the minimum amount of time. It would be disruptive to pull one away at such a critical moment, but they were essentially looking for a needle in a haystack, and if Strachey's idea would make it possible to cut to the chase, it might be worth trying.

"What's your idea, Vop?"

"It's so obvious it's probably wrong," began

the American, "but where would Zarin go to ground that he would consider safe and impervious to detection?"

Alberto immediately divined the answer.

"The embassy!"

He mentally chastised himself for having ordered José Solís to shut down the observation post on *Calle de Jerez*.

"*Me caga en la leche!* I fucked up! I told Solís to close the OP."

"That's too bad. I was wondering why we didn't have any new info from it. But still, do you agree it's worth a shot?"

"It's pretty farfetched to believe that the Iranians would be brazen enough to hide a nuclear weapon at their own embassy, but it's the only thing we have right now," said Alberto, still feeling deeply embarrassed about closing the observation post. "I'll get in touch with TEDAX immediately. There must be a van somewhere in the northern part of the city."

He went back upstairs to get on the line to the TEDAX command center.

They didn't like pulling one of their units from its designated route one bit and Alberto had to threaten to call in President Camisero before they agreed.

Just as he was coming back down the stairs to the lounge, he heard Strachey's cell phone shrill. The American's face registered disappointment as he listened to the call.

Snapping his phone shut, he said, "That

was Amy Dawson, our computer sorceress. She says there's no record of Zarin renting a car last night. We'd better have some more coffee."

Nearly an hour later, Gabriel Fonseca's lanky form appeared on the stairs and all eyes turned toward him.

"We found something," he announced. "A cabbie remembers taking a fare from the airport to *Calle de Jerez* around 8:00 P.M. There were two men. One was blond."

Alberto expelled a long sigh of relief.

"That gives us one part of the puzzle, and it means that the only person who can arm the second bomb is at the embassy. Now all we have to do is confirm the bomb is there."

*****

The Plutonium-239 contained in the Russian landmine emitted Alfa particles that were in and of themselves, undetectable. But the Alfa particles interacted with other matter. Radiation must be absorbed by ordinary matter in order to be detectable, and that interaction results in the separation of neutral atoms into negatively charged electrons and positively charged atoms that lack one or more electron. This is called ionization, and it is detectible in a number of ways.

As the TEDAX van drove slowly past the Iranian Embassy on *Calle de Jerez* the first indication of abnormal radioactivity was detected.

Ten minutes later a member of the NRBQ team passed the front of the embassy compound on foot. He wore a heavy coat that concealed a portable radiation detection device that fit around his upper body like a bulky vest. When he returned to the van and the data recorded by the device were analyzed, they knew they had found the bomb.

CHAPTER 44

"It isn't an ideal situation," said Harvey Grant rubbing the stubble on his cheek and feeling every one of his 60 years. "To state the obvious, Shirazi and the bomb are co-located."

"A single, well-placed missile could obliterate the entire compound," said Strachey.

"And that would risk setting off a dirty bomb," said Grant. "Radioactive materials could be dispersed over a very large area."

"That would still be better than a nuclear blast."

"I know you don't want to hear this, Bob, but think about the diplomatic consequences. If the compound, the sovereign territory of another country, were to be destroyed, likely killing everyone there, the Iranians would raise an international storm of protest, and we would have destroyed any evidence that would have justified such an action. And I guarantee that the politicians are thinking exactly the same thing right now. When all of this is over, one way or another, we will need proof of Iranian culpability so they can be held accountable."

"But we can't just sit around and wait for them to detonate the bomb."

"Correct. Welcome to the world of international politics where no decisions are easy and all of them have consequences."

Strachey made a sour face. "You know as well as I that no one is going to just sit back and let this thing happen, no matter the consequences. The Iranians are just crazy enough to detonate the damned bomb. If we've learned anything, it's that you can't negotiate with these bastards. There must be people in that compound, such as Zarin, who would gladly commit nuclear suicide."

They were speaking in English, but Alberto had managed to follow the conversation. "There's only one viable alternative," he said. "We'll have to storm the compound and secure the weapon by force before they can detonate it."

It was 6:00 A.M., and the winter sun would rise over Madrid in two hours.

*****

When Zarin led him into the chancery after viewing the bomb in the embassy garage and making certain it was guarded, Shirazi asked to see his family, but the Colonel refused. "They are safe enough," he said, "and will be leaving Madrid with the rest of the staff in a few days after Fernandez's ultimatum has been made public."

He locked Shirazi in a storage room in the garage where the man guarding the truck could keep an eye on him and then went to the ambassador's office where he turned on the television set and sat back to await the news. A little over two hours later the first reports of the declaration of a national state of emergency began to appear, and were soon confirmed. All flights had been grounded and ground travel was restricted to official vehicles. The government was not explaining the reason, and the news reporters were left to speculate about some sort of impending national catastrophe, perhaps a Chernobyl-style meltdown at one of Spain's several nuclear power plants.

Tendrils of doubt invaded Zarin's thoughts. Had the device malfunctioned? It was relatively antiquated, and a couple of decades old, and such was entirely possible. So far as he was aware, however, everything, with the notable exception of Shirazi's attempted perfidy, had gone exactly as planned. Thanks to Shirazi, the Spanish and the Americans would be aware that there was a plan to detonate a nuclear device in Spain, but Zarin had whisked Shirazi out of Madrid and Fernandez's agent had done a good job of confusing the issue. The authorities could know nothing more. Shirazi had known nothing about Fernandez or the targets and locations of the bombs.

For the time being there was nothing he could do but wait. Sooner or later news of the catastrophe in León would have to be reported. He remained glued to the television and as the hour was approaching 1:00 A.M. it came. According to the news bulletin, all communications with León had suddenly ceased. Calls to residences in outlying areas resulted in reports of a large flash in the sky, but all telephonic contact had shortly thereafter been cut off by the government.

Zarin finally relaxed. Success! He called the embassy communications technician to the office and composed a coded message to VEVAK headquarters that outlined his every heroic action, how he had taken control of the traitor Shirazi, calmed a nearly hysterical Miguel Fernandez, and himself driven the truck containing the bomb across nearly the entire country to León where he had forced the hapless Shirazi to arm it. He re-read and edited the message several times before he ordered it sent, and when the communications technician left, he stretched his body full length on the ambassador's sofa and dropped off to sleep, his dreams filled with images of a triumphal return to Tehran and the rewards that would be his.

CHAPTER 45

Checking his watch, Alberto realized there was little time left before the cover of darkness would be lost. The rim of the eastern sky would be turning gray in another hour as the pre-dawn approached.

Strachey said, "Alberto, we can have some of our best guys here in a couple of hours. We have Delta Force teams in forward locations all over Europe."

The Spaniard shook his head. "You and your people have done enough already. Without the assistance only you could have provided there would now be a smoking hole in the ground where León once stood. But this is a Spanish matter now. It is Spain that is threatened, and it's time for Spain to take care of her own."

"You're not going to leave me behind, Alberto. I want to be in at the finish."

The Spaniard regarded his American friend and wondered if his own face was equally haggard. "You've got it if you want it, *amigo*. I can't refuse you, but it's not going to be fun."

"You're the boss, Alberto. What do we do now?"

*****

The *Grupo Especial de Operaciones,* GEO was formed in 1978 in response to a wave of terrorism in Europe and violent terrorist acts in Spain committed by the Basque Separatist Group, ETA. GEO maintained its headquarters at Guadalajara, about 35 miles northwest of Madrid. The all-volunteer elite group of some 200 men scored countless operational successes against homegrown and foreign terrorists, including foiling a 1995 plot to assassinate the King of Spain, Juan Carlos I and the rescue from kidnappers of over 400 people, including the father of singer Julio Iglesias.

In its 31 years of existence, only one GEO had died in combat: in the assault on the Leganés apartment occupied by the perpetrators of the M-11 Madrid train bombings.

If they were to take advantage of the remaining darkness, the operational planners of the Christmas Day assault on the Iranian Embassy had little time. In fact, by the time the unit's Action Team 40, in dark overalls with balaclavas covering their faces, had begun to take up positions surrounding the compound, the sky was beginning to lighten. Fortunately, as part of the security preparations for the 1992 Barcelona Olympic Games, Spanish security had undertaken the complicated task of compiling and digitizing so-called "virtual reality" three dimensional architectural plans of the interiors of major buildings that would afford intervention forces with a preview of exactly what they would encounter when they entered a premises. Following the Olympics, the project was continued and expanded, and today Action Team 40 had an excellent idea of the internal layout of the embassy compound.

The compound was divided into two sections with multilevel living quarters in the west wing, including a large ambassadorial residence, and the chancery occupying the other wing that angled at 90 degrees toward *Calle de Jerez*. The L-shaped structure framed a large garden with a swimming pool at its center. The garage and maintenance areas were directly behind the chancery.

The Police Inspector who commanded Action Team 40 refused Alberto's request to be allowed to join in the assault, and the *Comisario Principal* had to agree that the man was correct. The team functioned as a harmonized unit with each member knowing precisely what the other members were doing at any given moment, and the insertion of an outsider would be disruptive, so as the assault began, Alberto and Strachey waited tensely in the mobile command post at the end of the block, their eyes glued to the monitors.

The plan was of necessity simple, given the short amount of time for preparation: the primary objective was the garage where they believed the bomb must be located. Simultaneously with the assault on the front gate, the living quarters would be secured by a team that would come over the west wall before the main assault was launched with the goal of minimizing potential casualties. There were some twenty permanent embassy staff members, including the ambassador, several with families, which would have to be accounted for and locked down. The number of security personnel and the number and type of weapons they might possess was unknown.

*****

Zarin was startled out of a sound sleep by a terrific bang outside the chancery, and he rushed to the window that faced the street. When he saw several armed men in black uniforms and balaclavas approaching the compound he immediately realized that they were after the bomb. *How did they know?* For just an instant he was seized by panic but it was quickly suppressed, and by the time the shooting began outside he knew what had to be done and that there would be no triumphal return to Tehran. He resolved that his holy mission would not fail, not now after everything he already had accomplished. If martyrdom was to be his fate, he would accept it gladly, and he would take hundreds of thousands of the infidels with him in a swirling cauldron of atomic fire.

As he pounded down the stairs from the ambassador's office to the rear of the building, he could hear the guard he had left with the truck returning the attackers' fire. There was a covered passage leading from the chancery to an entrance in the side of the garage and he headed for it now. Once inside he would secure a weapon from the embassy's arms locker at the rear of the maintenance area. He knew that the other two security guards had their quarters over the garage and the suddenly increased intensity of the gunfire outside now told him that they too had engaged the attackers. They were armed with Heckler & Koch MP5 submachine guns and should be able to prevent the garage from being taken before Zarin could complete his plan.

Across the street a pre-positioned GEO sniper took careful aim at the garage's second story window from which his team was taking concentrated fire and acquired his target. He squeezed the trigger of his SAKO TRG-41 sniper rifle, and its deadly .338 Lapua Magnum round found its mark. Firing from the window ceased for a moment but was soon resumed by another shooter. The sniper squinted through his sight and waited patiently for his chance.

A helicopter swooped low over the compound, coming to a hover above the roof of the living quarters, and four GEO's deployed down ropes and took up positions overlooking the garden. Two of them made their way carefully toward the roof of the garage.

Inside, seeing that the guard by the truck was still returning fire, Zarin hailed him and ran for the weapons locker where he retrieved another H&K and two grenades. He then unlocked the storage room where Shirazi had been confined and dragged him out.

A bewildered Shirazi found himself being shoved toward the familiar truck in the semi-darkness of garage's interior, the barrel of Zarin' weapon planted painfully in the small of his back, as bullets whined through the air and impacted on the walls, other parked vehicles, and pinged off of heavy equipment.

Sheltering behind the truck, Zarin shouted, "You will arm the bomb NOW, before we are overrun. Complete your mission, Major Shirazi, and perhaps God will forgive you." He leaned around the back of the truck and squeezed off several rounds before turning back to face a petrified Shirazi.

"NOW, Major," he shouted savagely, "Get into the truck and get to work!" and he brought the H&K back around to point it at Shirazi's mid-section. "Forget about your safeties and pre-checks. The bomb must be detonated before we're overrun!"

Shirazi climbed mechanically up into the bed of the truck where he crouched next to the ugly gray shape of the five-ton Russian landmine.

MICHAEL R. DAVIDSON

He picked up the wrench and began removing the bolts that held the access panel in place. Within half a minute he swung it open to expose the trigger mechanism.

An explosion ripped through the upper story of the garage from a hand grenade tossed through the open window by one of the GEO's who had crawled over the roof and dangled dangerously over the side, his legs held by his comrade. At the same time the attackers tossed smoke grenades outside and advanced toward the open garage doors, spraying automatic fire from their SG 552 Commando carbines.

The guard was pinned down under a hail of bullets, and some rounds ripped into the front of the truck and through the canvas that was stretched over the metal ribs covering the cargo area. Some pinged off the bomb casing. Shirazi dove for cover behind the device. As one GEO emerged from the smoke, the guard rose to fire at him but was cut down by a blast from the Franchi shotgun carried by another GEO.

Zarin hunkered behind the truck as the smoke cleared and the firing ceased. He wasn't certain that they knew he was there. "Get it going, Major," he rasped, "we have only seconds left. Forget the diagnostics – just set it off!" He tossed one of his grenades toward the front of the garage and clambered into the truck to stand over Shirazi. The lead GEO's didn't have a chance as shrapnel from the blast shredded flesh and bone, and those behind immediately sought cover.

Zarin had bought them some time and wondered if he could use his remaining grenade to detonate the explosives packed around the bomb's nuclear core to create a dirty bomb. This, he decided, he would do if Shirazi faltered.

*****

Shirazi's mind had begun to function again and the image of his family flashed before his eyes. They were still here in the embassy and would be incinerated along with thousands of other innocent people if he armed the bomb. The Iranian Major had accepted the inevitability of his own death and an eternity in hell for the blood already on his hands, but now Zarin was asking too much.

"No, Colonel Zarin," he said through bared teeth, an animal growl rising to his throat from some recess deep inside, "I won't do it again!" He stood up quickly and brandished the heavy wrench.

Zarin was startled and stepped quickly back from Shirazi raising his H&K as he did so, but one foot went over the back of the truck bed and he tumbled to fall hard onto the concrete floor, losing the weapon in the impact. With Zarin momentarily stunned Shirazi leapt from the truck and was on top of the blond colonel before he could regain his feet. Lifting the wrench high above his head, Shirazi brought it down with all his strength into the colonel's face, shattering the man's nose and one eye socket with a sickening crunch. His face contorted with the rage that energized his limbs as he smashed the wrench repeatedly into Zarin' head until brains and blood spread across the floor.

He was still mechanically lifting and lowering the heavy tool when the GEO's moved cautiously into the garage and around the truck and restrained him.

*****

Alberto and Strachey bolted from the rear of the mobile command post as soon as the GEO team leader confirmed that the assault was over. They ran the length of the block to the gates of the embassy that were now dangling from their hinges at odd angles, arriving at the same time as Paco Mendoza and his TEDAX team, and they went into the garage together.

Alberto was shocked as he walked past the torn bodies of the two GEO's who had led the assault, one of them the team leader. Inside they discovered Shirazi held securely between two GEO's as he stared with hysterical, wide eyes at the battered corpse that had only moments earlier been Colonel Aref Zarin of *the Vezarat-e Ettela'at va Amniat-e Keshvar*. Zarin lay sprawled on the cement floor with a widening pool of blood encircling the fractured remains of his head.

Paco Mendoza whistled them over to the back of the truck where the Russian nuclear landmine, its rear access hatch still open, could be seen.

"It was a close thing," said Mendoza.

Alberto, his eyes fixed on the bomb, wondered out loud, "How twisted must a person be ever even to contemplate detonating such a monstrous weapon in the midst of innocent people?" He stared down at Zarin' corpse. "What kind of aberrant belief breeds monsters like this? I can understand Fernandez's motives up to a point, but what could have driven the Iranians to such insane lengths?"

Strachey laid his hand on the Spaniard's shoulder. "And I wonder how many more times we'll have to go to such desperate lengths to stop them before someone decides to go after the infection at its source."

The Spaniard embraced his American friend. "Thank you for sticking with me."

"You call any time, Alberto, and I'll be there."

CHAPTER 46

The secret facility, built originally with CIA funds and intended to house and interrogate captured illegal foreign combatants, was tucked into a fold in the hills outside Zaragoza, about 180 miles northeast of Madrid. Inside, Alberto Macías sat facing Miguel Fernandez in the latter's cell where their conversation was taking a familiar and tiresome turn.

"What of the injustices, the genocide, inflicted upon my people? An entire population uprooted, dispossessed, expelled from their own land all in the name of a so-called 'Prince of Peace?' What of those who were tortured in the most bestial manner and killed, all to satisfy the avarice of the Church and its sadistic servants? What do you think of that, *Comisario*?"

"I think it was a long time ago, Fernandez, and civilization has progressed considerably since then."

"You miss the point, *Comisario*. I would

have restored *Al Andaluz* and the tolerant civilization that once thrived under the Caliphate. I would have returned Islam to its rightful place in Europe and displayed to the world its superiority over the decadence that now besets what you call 'civilization.'"

"Fernandez, you're just another fanatic thug whose idea of 'tolerance' is to kill anyone who disagrees with you."

"My goal was to right a terrible wrong."

"So say all terrorists, from Lenin to Hitler to the IRA to ETA to Al Qaeda, not to mention your Iranian friends. But nothing justifies mass murder. You blame others for your own shortcomings, for the failings of your distant ancestors. People like you do nothing but pick at ancient wounds to keep them festering while you ignore the fact that the world has moved on."

"Look at the poverty in the Islamic world today, the misery, the injustices. Do you call that 'moving on'?"

"I call that too much power in the hands of too few and a refusal to accept modernity. It's too easy for you to generalize and leave out the inconvenient facts."

Fernandez again snorted his contempt while Alberto continued, "You say you want to establish a 'tolerant' society and yet you fail utterly to recognize that you already live in one. I can understand the fears of your ancestors 500, 200, even 100 years ago, but now, in today's Spain, there is nothing that would have prevented you from declaring your true faith and your heritage. Your professed belief in a more tolerant Islam would have been welcomed, and you would have had considerable influence. Instead, whereas your ancestors were persecuted by a medieval Church and its Inquisition, you chose to align yourself with today's purveyors of medieval religious intolerance."

Fernandez smiled archly. "It's not over."

CHAPTER 47

Strachey sat across a starched white tablecloth from Amy Dawson who had forsaken her geeky black horn rimmed glasses in favor of contact lenses and exchanged the demur pantsuit she normally wore to the office for a sequined red dress and three inch Stuart Weitzman pumps. The sight of this transformed creature had taken Strachey's breath away and turned the heads even of the tuxedoed waiters as they entered the venerable Prime Rib restaurant on 'K' Street.

They were waiting for desert following a sumptuous meal. Strachey had been gratified by the enthusiasm with which the slender CIA computer whiz tucked into her rare New York strip steak. The absence of quality cuts of beef was the single weak spot he had discovered in Spanish cuisine. The bottle of 1989 Chateau Petrus that had cost Strachey a half-week's pay but had proven to be a perfect accompaniment to the meat, and both now settled into the glowing contentment that an excellent meal in charming company can provide.

"So where is Shirazi now?" asked Amy.

Ops folk didn't usually share such info with Directorate of Intelligence folk, but in this case Strachey didn't mind. Amy had earned her spurs, as had an unexpectedly robust and resourceful Harvey Grant. "We have him and his family in a safehouse out in Fairfax County," he said. "He was nearly a total mental case when they pulled him off Zarin. He was convinced he had already murdered the population of León and that he was going to hell, and collapsed completely when Alberto told him that the city was still standing. The poor bastard went through a lot. He's a goldmine of information on the Iranian nuclear weapons program."

"Nevertheless, he DID light the fuse in León."

"Yeah, but if it hadn't been for him in the first place, they would have carried off the whole damned crazy plot that Fernandez dreamed up."

"What a story - over half a millennium in the making. What do you think they'll do to Fernandez?"

"Oh, he'll never see the light of day again as long as he lives. To avoid a trial and all the questions that would be raised, they quietly had him declared insane (not a bad call, by the way) and locked him up where no one will ever find him. They would have done the same with

Sevillano, but when the GEO boys learned that some of their comrades had been killed during the embassy assault, the good police Director suffered a fatal accident en route to Madrid. He apparently forgot to fasten his seatbelt and fell out of a helicopter. Fortunately for his wife, she had no idea what he was up to. Apparently, the *Hermandad* members eventually had to start marrying nice Catholic girls when the supply of Muslim maidens went dry in Spain. They kept that part of their lives completely separate, except for the eldest sons, who were initiated into the secret brotherhood when they reached their teens. It was strictly a boys' club."

"Ergo 'brotherhood' like the Muslim Brotherhood in Egypt."

"Something like that, but several centuries older."

"I guess it was inevitable that the press would find out about the bombs," she sighed.

As Alberto had anticipated, the fact that the Iranians had tried to plant nuclear bombs in Spain had leaked to the press, although the government miraculously had managed to keep the Fernandez part of the story under wraps. What happened in León had to be explained, and there were too many people who recognized the effects of an electromagnetic pulse. Also, Harvey Grant had pointed out that laying the entire blame on the Iranians, i.e. a sovereign government, for concocting a nuclear plot offered more benefit than attributing it to a bunch of home grown terrorists, and the Spanish were happy to cooperate. It provided the perfect justification for an assault on the embassy of a foreign country.

In the aftermath, the Islamic Republic had reverted to form and taken the staff of the Spanish Embassy in Tehran hostage and threatened to put them on trial. They appeared to have forgotten that the Spanish already had in custody the staff of the Iranian Embassy in Madrid and were armed with incontrovertible evidence of the two bombs, which made the accusation of Iran's culpability impossible for the mullahs to refute. The Spanish legitimately could put the embassy staff on trial for terrorism. This episode had the added benefit of making the Iranians even greater international pariahs than ever, and the U.S. at last had some real allies in their efforts to isolate the regime of the mullahs. In the end, Iran agreed to exchange their hostages for the staff of their Madrid embassy.

Before returning to Washington for debriefings, Strachey and Grant had enjoyed a reunion with Alberto (now elevated by President Camisero to the position of sub-director of the CNP), Gordi (who made a great show of limping in with the aid of a cane), and the irrepressible Nicolas Villagas (who still complained that no one had given him a gun). They had met in the comfortable *Restaurante Cristobal* in Alberto's native Sepúlveda, and Grant was still talking about the roast lamb and convivial atmosphere.

They had all stared in fascination at the ancient Moorish dagger Alberto brought for them to see.

Strachey was looking forward to returning to Madrid.

"What about the other members of the *Hermandad*?" asked Amy.

"Dunno.   Allegedly all of them except Fernandez and Sevillano left the country to wait for the great day and their triumphal return. They're still somewhere in North Africa for all anybody knows, but Alberto is heading up an investigation, and if anybody can find the bastards, he can."

"I hope so. He sounds very resourceful."

Strachey looked speculatively across the table as the waiter served dessert, "You ought to meet him sometime, Amy. How would you like to visit Spain?"

EPILOGUE – The End of the World

Miguel Fernandez, as his father had instructed, left Spain as soon as Shirazi's treachery had become known.

Now, long after nightfall, he stood on a sandy beach in Morocco gazing northward where he could see the lights of Tarifa glowing on Spain's Costa de la Luz across the Straits of Gibraltar. He feared he would never return to the land of his birth, and he wept for the lost Al Andaluz.

THE END

Afterword

The scene described at the beginning of the book ("Lighting the Fuse") is said actually to have happened as Abu Abdullah, known popularly in modern Spain as "Boabdil," left Granada and paused in the mountain pass known to this day as *"El Último Suspiro del Moro,"* (The Moor's Last Sigh). 1492 was a pivotal year in Spanish history in which three important events occurred: the final re-conquest of Spain after 700 years of Moorish rule, the expulsion of the Jews, and the discovery of the New World. The historical Miguel Fernandez was, in fact, the illegitimate offspring of King Fernando and the daughter of Boabdil. What actually happened to Fernandez and his progeny is lost in the mists of history, and references to them in this story are purely fictional.

MRD

MICHAEL R. DAVIDSON

The prequel to "Retribution"[4]

In 1492 victorious King Fernando of Aragon forces the daughter of the last Muslim ruler in Andalusia to become his concubine as a gesture of "reconciliation." The product of their coupling, a secret Muslim with an abiding hatred for his father, founds a line that nurtures the flame of vengeance through the centuries.

Disillusioned by Spain's failing fortunes in the 30-Years-War, Eduardo Macías leaves the Army of Flanders and sets out for home. Eduardo's reputation as a valorous soldier leads to his being named Captain of the Santa Hermandad, a Spanish force charged with protecting the people and maintaining the law. He is forced to accept a mission by officials of the Holy Inquisition to investigate an alleged case of heresy involving a nobleman with ancient royal ties. What Eduardo discovers places him in a dangerous situation at odds with the Inquisition, and he must choose between upholding his honor and excommunication.

---

[4] 2nd edition, available at Amazon.com in paperback and Kindle forms, Copyright © 2012 by Michael R. Davidson

---

The Author

Michael R. Davidson was raised in the Mid-West. Heeding President Kennedy's call for more young Americans to learn Russian he studied the language, and military service took him to the White House where he served as translator for the Moscow-Washington "Hotline." His language abilities attracted the attention of the Central Intelligence Agency, and following his military service Mr. Davidson spent the next 28 years as a Clandestine Services officer. Seventeen of those years were spent abroad in a variety of sensitive posts working against the Soviet Union and the Warsaw Pact. In the private sector he worked as a business owner and security and economic development consultant before devoting full time to his writing.

Also by Michael R. Davidson

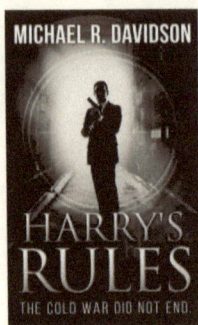

Did the Cold War end or did the KGB find a way to retain its power and dominate the new Russian Federation? "Harry's Rules" is an espionage thriller set against the backdrop of post-Soviet Russia in the early 1990's.

Who killed President John F. Kennedy? A long buried secret that could change the course of history draws murder to a quiet Washington suburb. Only an exiled CIA officer can solve a mystery that both the White House and the Kremlin will protect at all costs.

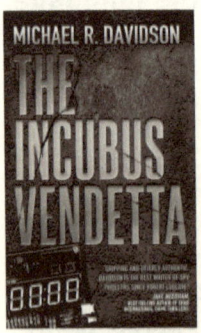

Revenge is said to be a dish best served cold. A suicide bomber and a serial killer are the instruments chosen by a deposed Russian president.

But his targets are anything but helpless.

Find them all at: www.michaelrdavidson.com
All books also available at Amazon.com

KRYSTAL - **Sassy** Detective Krystal Murphy who appeared in INCUBUS and THE INCUBUS VENDETTA at last gets her own novel.

A controversial Miami judge is murdered in a Washington hotel room. Homicide detective Krystal Murphy identifies an ideal suspect, a person with motive and opportunity. Following the suspect's trail to Miami, she is confronted by an unspeakable tragedy that leaves her prime suspect dead. Convinced her initial instincts were wrong and driven by guilt, she teams with a Miami detective to continue the investigation. But she encounters unexpected opposition from her own superiors who want only to call the case closed. While coping with her own personal tragedy and under great pressure from her superiors, Krystal doggedly pursues the case with the help a new ally and perhaps more than just a friend, the Miami detective. When more people associated with the case begin turning up dead, Krystal finds herself in a race against time before she herself becomes the next victim of an increasingly desperate killer.

Find them all at: www.michaelrdavidson.com
All books also available at Amazon.com

MICHAEL R. DAVIDSON

COMING SOON!!

IN THE
SHADOW OF
MORDOR
MICHAEL R. DAVIDSON
KSENIYA KIRILLOVA

**Michael R. Davidson teams with
Russian author Kseniya Kirillova
to pen a tale torn from the realities
of today's Russia.**